CANTONELLI'S CREST

PURPLE HAVEN

To Leah—
Enjoy every bite!
Angel Musk
xoxo

ANGEL MUSK

Editing by: Alisha Marie Carnes

Cover Art by: Brandi Doane McCann

Illustration by: Michael Musk

author HOUSE®

AuthorHouse™
1663 Liberty Drive
Bloomington, IN 47403
www.authorhouse.com
Phone: 1 (800) 839-8640

Published by AuthorHouse 04/15/2016

ISBN: 978-1-5049-8597-0 (sc)
ISBN: 978-1-5049-8578-9 (hc)
ISBN: 978-1-5049-8596-3 (e)

Library of Congress Control Number: 2016904366

Print information available on the last page.

This book is printed on acid-free paper.

CHAPTER ONE

Grant Biltmore tossed and turned in his exquisite four-pillared bed as horrific images interfered his sleep. Feeling the piercing needles that prodded his neck, seeing the large amount of blood and the metallic smell trapped in the air felt very real to him. Eyes tightly closed and sweat cascading from his forehead, he leaned over the side of his bed and vomited. After purging last night's chili dinner, he lay flat on his back and watched the blades on the ceiling fan turn slowly until the spasms in his stomach retreated. He had never been a dreamer or, if he was, never remembered them, but the human monsters he saw in his sleep rattled him to the core.

The way their bodies moved at lightning speed was off the charts of any scientific measurement that he knew of and those purple eyes were so captivating they could make anyone do anything. This dream was getting the best of him. Realizing it was Tuesday and he needed to get to the hospital, he pushed the silver button on his bedroom wall that automatically opened the window blinds to assess the weather. He showered, then dressed himself using the elongated mirror to perfect his tie. His work schedule that afternoon was filled with back to back meetings and he also had power point slides to review before hand, but his mind was preoccupied by unrealistic characters. Adjusting his tie, he noticed how healthy he looked. The dark circles that had been under his eyes for months were gone and his boney sunken in cheeks were once again rosy and vibrant. His hair looked fuller just as it did when he was younger. He couldn't believe the man he saw staring back at him. The experimental treatment must have worked!

****

...the day before

Grant was the chief operating officer of the XL Auto Company located in his hometown of Adora Valley, Colorado. His business partner, Ethan, thought using abbreviations made the company more "hip" to advertise. Xtreme Luxury vehicles was formed fifteen years ago when they were fresh out of college and were lucky enough to find an investor interested in their business plan. They had worked hard and tripled their profits by the ten-year mark by making average vehicles into a lavish and safe transportation option. Some clients wanted comfort and other clients needed vehicles with advanced safety measures, depending on their social status. Very reputable and wealthy clients helped it flourish into a multi-million dollar company.

Finished for the day, and the last to leave the office, he turned off the building lights and waited patiently for the elevator to take him to his red Ferrari in the parking garage. As he loosened up his tie he pushed a button on the key fob which popped open the door and placed his briefcase securely behind the passenger seat. Climbing in the driver seat, he pushed a button which started the ignition and then took a quick assessment at himself in the rear view mirror. Another day down and none of his employees noticed the weight loss, melancholy, or general weakness. His secret of having cancer was safe for now.

Four months ago he had been diagnosed with cancer, and it was progressing at an alarming rate. Researchers in Sweden were in the last phases of developing a treatment drug that would increase the survival rate in patients with his type of terminal illness by twenty percent. Grant agreed to participate in a clinical trial as long as it was confidential. A local doctor approved by the drug sponsor monitored his progress and obtained weekly blood samples at the local hospital. He was identified as study participant 0986 so reports did not state his full name and information.

After work on Mondays, he always frequented his favorite restaurant, Sky Chili. It killed his acid reflux, but he had grown up on the famous local chili so his body always craved it. As Grant steered his car toward the exit of the work parking garage, he noticed a large van behind him, which seemed odd that anyone else would be on the premises after eight o'clock. Reaching his destination twenty minutes later, he parked, then pressed the button on his dash to stop the engine. He had a passion for cars since high school and loved the modern technology placed in vehicles these days. The perks of his job gave him opportunities to try out the latest gadgets before they were available on the market. Activating the alarm on his car, he realized the same van from the parking garage was parked right next to him. *Surely he wasn't being followed?*

Inside the restaurant, watching the Wildcats basketball game on the flat screen TV and three coney dogs later he went to the men's room to clean up a stain on his brand new tie. As Grant stood at the sink meticulously scrubbing away at his tie, two men dressed in black leather coats entered the room and stood right behind Grant with their arms folded.

"Sorry fellas, I'll be just a minute. Seems my tie is a magnet for chili," Grant said, oblivious to their surly demeanor. After that encounter Grant Biltmore would never be the same again.

CHAPTER TWO

Before work every Tuesday morning, Grant went to the hospital diligently for vital sign and blood level checks. He knew the phlebotomists by name and jokingly called them blood suckers. The four tubes of blood collected would be analyzed and the results sent to his research doctor for review. By one o'clock, he would get the routine phone call reporting any progression from last week. Usually, the outcome was the same as last week.

It was after lunch when Grant was finalizing his power point slide on ergonomics of interior design in automobiles when he received the call of his lab results. This time the news was definitely not what he expected to hear.

"Mr. Biltmore, your blood test results came back with something I've never seen before in my thirty-eight years of medicine," Dr. Rowland announced with his gravelly voice.

Grant rose from his desk and quickly shut his office door for privacy then took the phone off of speaker.

"Go on please," Grant said curiously.

"Your coagulation results came back erroneous so I had them rechecked...twice. The prothrombin time reported extremely low," Dr. Rowland stated with concern.

Grant was in no way medically knowledgeable and had no idea what those words even remotely meant. He heard his employees' voices in the faint distance and realized they must be returning from lunch and anticipated the two o'clock operations meeting would soon begin.

"Doctor, what exactly are you trying to say? I'm sorry for my boldness but I have a meeting starting in fifteen minutes," Grant said anxiously.

He didn't mean to sound rude but he believed that personal life should be separated from business and did not want his employees to overhear his medical information. His eyes darted from cubicle to cubicle outside his windows to ensure nobody was approaching his door. Mona, his secretary had a habit of entering without knocking even though he repeatedly told her to announce herself before entering.

"Grant, the level was a 0.0, which is impossible. That would mean all of the blood in your veins has clotted and there is no pass through for oxygen or nutrients to your main organs. That is not the only reason why I am baffled. Your vital sign record in your chart from this morning's visit was…immeasurable. I even spoke to the CNA personally on the phone to get the accurate reading. She explained that she used several devices to get a reading and none of them worked. She admitted they had been bombarded with stat blood draw requests so she did not press the issue as you were clearly functional," he explained.

Grant's stomach began to flip flop, his hands shook and nearly dropped the receiver. He was more confused with every word the doctor spoke. To make matters worse, Mona appeared at his window, motioning that she wanted to come in. He immediately shook his head no and held up his index finger as a sign for her to wait. Luckily, she nodded and returned to her desk without any further interruption. Holding the receiver in his left hand, he lowered his forehead on his right palm balancing his upper body with his elbow resting on the polished mahogany desk.

"Your pulse rate was zero. Your blood pressure was zero over zero and your oxygen level was…zero. Grant, to put it in simple terms, it appears you are clinically dead according to the standards of general medicine. Now I've contacted the medical monitor of the case study you are participating in and…."

Grant dropped the phone after he heard the man say, "dead" and began to shake uncontrollably. Visions of his dream the night before flashed in his mind like a thirty-second horror film. Those men in the bathroom at Sky Chili must have done something to him. The dream was real. As if his brain finally allowed him to remember, he remembered cleaning the stain from his tie as the two strangers stood behind him staring at him intently. Before Grant could turn the water off they were on top of him restraining his arms to the ground. Grant's strength was no match for theirs so he had no choice but to let them mug him. Faded images of being carried out into a black vehicle with tinted windows validated his reasoning. He remembered that the inside of the vehicle was custom made and disguised into a mobile ambulance. The interior paneling was impressively elegant with top quality materials only available from Italy so he was sure that his company did not build that vehicle. He must have blacked out after his capture because his next memory was waking up in his bed at home as if nothing even happened.

"Hello? Grant, are you still there?" Dr. Rowland asked repeatedly.

Grant raised the receiver back up to his ear to answer the doctor when someone pressed the hook on the phone causing a dial tone to sound. Someone just hung up his call! *Damn it, Mona.* He was about to reprimand his secretary for her rudeness when he looked up and saw a man dressed in black wearing a red cape, with a sleek yet muscular build, brown wavy hair, and purple eyes. Standing next to the mysterious visitor was a tall, skinny, attractive woman with choppy blonde hair spiked in every direction. She also had purple eyes.

"You need to come with us, Mr. Biltmore," the brawny man said. Grant suddenly realized the strange people had returned for him and attempted a rushed exit toward his private side door. "Elise, now!" the man commanded.

Grant had almost reached the doorknob when suddenly he no longer had control of his body. As if in an imaginary bubble, he felt his body turn around facing his guests and was stunned to see the woman's eyes glowing. She was extremely focused on Grant as if they were the only people in the room. His legs began to walk on their own toward her, and he realized she was controlling his mind and body. *This cannot be happening. Creatures like this only exist in the Marvel Comics.*

The man spoke in a deep authoritative voice, "Take him, and I will meet you at the estate."

Following his orders, she silently commanded Grant's body to get inside the waiting vehicle and surprisingly she fastened his seat belt. *Surely if they were going to kill me, she wouldn't have thought about safety.*

Once they were on the road, the locks automatically bolted on the inside of each car door to trap him in, the woman released her hold of Grant's mind so she could keep her eyes on the road. Grasping the steering wheel with both hands she listened to his erratic thoughts and waited for his brazened moment of anger. She kind of felt sorry for him and thought he was very attractive. He was definitely tugging at her heart strings. She then giggled to herself and thought, *if I had a beating heart.*

"Who in the hell are you people and where are you taking me?" Grant shouted in disbelief.

"Mr. Biltmore, I know you have a lot of questions but unfortunately I am not the one who should answer them. The place we are going holds the answer to every question you may produce. I can assure you we wish you no harm. Please accept my apologies as we had no time for introductions back there. My name is Elise Cantonelli," she said soothingly to her handsome assignment.

Since when are kidnappers respectful? Try respectful and gorgeous. He studied her while she drove trying to think how he could escape but he did not feel she would hurt him. Strangely, he wanted to know more about her. Grant decided he was not saying another word until he spoke to the person in charge of this heist. After all he was a rich executive and knew how to facilitate "persistent" people.

Elise felt Grant's thoughts overwhelming her, and the goose bumps on her temples were proof. She had never gotten used to the feeling of hearing a person's thoughts and soon she would have to silence Mr. Biltmore. The gift of mind control was a luxury most vampires had, however it only worked on the opposite sex. That was why immortals always worked in pairs, one man and one woman. Despite extensive research, nobody could ever figure out why vampires could not control people of the same sex. The feeling of being in love could never be forced upon a person. Many vampires have tried in the past but love was a power too strong to be controlled. Socially and romantically, this was a blessing in disguise.

Elise heard him think of her as gorgeous and it made her smile but then sighed loudly at the annoying twinge at her temples and needed silence. It was time to shut Mr. Biltmore down for a while. She abruptly turned the wheel to the right and pulled the vehicle over to the shoulder. Her erratic move made Grant wonder if his captor was psychotic. Hearing his assumption of her, she angrily turned to face Grant's direction. *Oh, crap.* Elise conjured her energy and he watched her eyes transition to a luminous color of purple. His honey-colored eyes grew wide as quarters and opened his mouth to yell for help as fear took over his body. Something bad was going to happen. She stared at him as she parted her lips and released an iridescent fog that encircled his face as she whispered, "Sleep."

His body immediately slumped forward and his arms fell limp. Ah…peace at last. She turned her attention back on the road. Flipping her turn signal on, she steered the vehicle into the appropriate lane and then her cell phone began to ring. Her caller identification read, Santiago.

"Hello? Yes, I've got him and everything is fine. No, I do not need your assistance. I will call you if I do," Elise said angrily as she ended the phone call.

Gripping the steering wheel tighter in frustration as she drove, she decided to turn the radio on for distraction. Music always soothed her soul when she was in the worst of moods. The radio station was in the middle of playing Bad Suns song, *"Cardiac Arrest"* and she rolled her eyes at the irony of the situation making her wonder what true love would feel like. After a few minutes she rolled her eyes and changed the channel and Katy Perry's new song, "*Dark Horse*" had just come on. The beat of that song was an instant mood enhancer. Singing the verses like the pro she was, she scanned her rear-view mirrors to make sure nobody from Grant's office was following her. They had made sure they exited swiftly without any of his employees noticing anything, but you never knew for sure until a gawker caught up with you and tried to cut your head off. Now that had been a scary experience to go through after just being turned. She was not letting that happen again.

She turned around to check on her handsome guest in the back seat. Turning immortal definitely worked in his favor. As she suspected, he was sleeping like a baby. The sleep charm as immortals called it only lasted for thirty minutes or so. Upon awakening, the individual remained in an amnesia state, so they did not recall any events that occurred during their slumber. It was very helpful when dealing with uncooperative mortals and immortals. It had been the easiest charm to learn when she became a vampire and since then she had conquered the most complicated of charms.

Remembering her last phone call from her uncle's enforcers caused her to feel guilty about her rudeness toward them. After all, Santiago and Lucas were just making sure their assignment was near completion. They had initiated the first contact with Grant and were responsible for a successful turn. Sighing, she realized she would need to apologize later to them. She understood their concern, considering she was just returning to work after the "almost becoming headless" ordeal, which had caused her to lose a lot of blood. If the enforcer's hadn't been in the area that night and sought help for her right away after she was attacked, she would have been dust in the wind.

****

Elise turned down the stone paved road and was almost to the entrance of the estate. It brought back memories of the first time she had been there and was astonished by the massive brick dwelling that sat on almost five hundred acres of woods. She had grown up in the area but never knew the place existed until the day she took her last breath as a mortal and suddenly it became her home. The estate looked as if it belonged to a governor or person of high stature due to the security and ridiculous screening protocols. However, it was all necessary to conceal their nature of existence and preserve what they had developed since the sixteenth century.

Noticing the men on alert and stationed at the large metal gate, she sent a telepathic message to them. *It's Elise with a newly turned. Please open the gates and alert the enforcers.*

Seconds later, the men stepped out of the way while talking into their security headpieces to deliver the message as she accelerated up the driveway. Driving around to the back entrance as per newly-turned protocol, she checked the rear-view mirror to make sure the gates had closed successfully behind her. Safety was important to her family's survival and occasionally Rogue immortals tried to surpass their barriers. Suddenly, she heard a moan from the back-seat and realized

Grant was starting to wake. The garage door opened automatically and her uncle and his men were waiting, ready to complete their mission. Her uncle had arrived moments before she had. She parked the vehicle inside then the doors began to immediately close behind her while the men rushed to the vehicle.

"He's just starting to wake up. We better get him situated quickly," she announced.

Nodding their heads, the two enforcers opened the car doors and lifted Grant up as if he weighed less than a feather and carried him into the mansion. Elise noticed the enforcers wouldn't look her in the eyes, and she felt ashamed for her behavior on the phone earlier. Her uncle Roman, noticed the tension between them and stepped forward, wrapping his arm around her shoulder, listening intently to her thoughts.

Her uncle was more like a father to her and always comforted her when she needed it. She didn't know of the family secret until last year when she was turned. After she had been bitten by a rogue vampire, Roman had sat her down and explained everything. The news answered many of the lingering questions she had about him as a child. She then understood why her uncle always donned a Kevlar vest and red velvet hooded cape. The vest was to stop any penetration to his heart, such as a stake or cross, and the hood to block the sun.

"You have done well. How does it feel to be back to work?" he asked, already knowing of her tense phone conversation.

Roman was very intuitive and knew things almost before they happened. It was a wonderful trait to have as long as she was not the center of it. He was almost 470 years old and was the eldest in the Cantonelli family. He held high honor and respect from all immortals globally. His love for his family was evident, and he worked day and night to make sure they were safe from rogues and mortals who knew too much.

"It felt nice to get out and about. I didn't realize how bored I was, sitting around waiting to heal from my attacker. Although I need to apologize to Lucas and Santiago for...well, I'm sure you already know what happened," Elise said solemnly.

Smiling in acknowledgment, Roman walked her to the main sitting room, where he had blood warmed and ready for her to drink after her first mission since being attacked. He motioned toward the long-stemmed glass giving her permission to partake and watched her sit in the long-backed cushioned chair near the fireplace. After a couple of minutes, the glass was empty and Elise was licking her lips in contentment. She knew her part of the assignment was over and the enforcers would take over the newly turned to begin the final transformation. Some newly-turned vampires took the news very well and others had to be relinquished and mind warped. She felt sorry for the new vampire, as she had once been in his position and had to make a choice.

"I'm glad to hear that you are eager to return to work, as I have a new assignment for you," her uncle announced confidently.

"Sure, uncle, anything for you. After all, I would not be here if you had not saved my life," she respectfully said.

Roman knew that his next command would not sit well with her. Although he was a man of power, he had a soft spot for his dear niece and valued her opinion. He would never show it, of course, because that would be a sign of weakness. However, his premonitions told him that new opportunities had arrived for her that was important for vampires all over the world and could not be ignored.

"Lucas and Santiago are leaving in the morning to California to check on our blood supply, and diffuse a situation that occurred. They will be gone for a couple days which means I need you to assist Mr. Biltmore with understanding his new lifestyle, if he agrees to the rules. Since you became a part of our immortal family just last year, I think you would be the most understanding person to guide him. He will relate to you easier than to anyone else," he explained.

Elise could not believe he was asking this of her. She was a trained enforcer, not a nanny. What about her singing career and album release? She also had to prepare for the private concert for the Countess of Corona in Canada, per her agent. If Elise was alive, her life would be over.

"I sense resistance to your new assignment. Care to explain?" her uncle asked boldly. He paced back and forth in front of the fireplace with his back turned to her, hiding his smile as he heard her thoughts. Although she was twenty-nine, singing was priority in her life and she was quickly rising to fame.

She understood he had already stated his orders and she could not revoke them. He was in charge, and she saw the things that happened when immortals did not do as he said. Being on his good side was her daily strategy and during stressful times his temper did get out of control. Roman heard her thoughts and straightened his posture then turned to face her. *Busted.*

"Uncle, I am willing to help in your time of need. However, I do not feel I am prepared for this assignment. I also have a contractual music obligation with Crimson Records to release two albums a year in which both are far from being finished. Besides, I do not know Mr. Biltmore and cannot gauge how he will react to this new lifestyle. If I have to relinquish him...I don't think I could do it," Elise wearily admitted. She stood up and began to pour herself a glass of wine from the bar, avoiding his gaze.

Relinquishing was a grueling task of basically erasing a person's existence by using charms, intense meditation, and mind control. It was a sad process watching someone waste away to nothing as if they never stepped foot on the universe. The emotional toll it caused the person performing it left them with weakened brain activity and physically defenseless against Rogue's for the next couple hours. Not to mention the fact of coping with destroying someone off the face of the earth.

"I will be the only one performing the relinquishing if it comes down to that. Although, I have no doubt that Mr. Biltmore will agree to his new life and will achieve great things for our family. As for your concert, it will need to be pushed back. I will call your manager, Talion at Crimson Records and explain that I need you here due to a family issue. As a matter of fact, I will personally call the Countess of Corona and apologize for the need of rescheduling her private entertainment. The Countess and I have had a friendship since we met over a hundred years ago. I will use this as an opportunity to catch up."

Who was this Mr. Biltmore who captivated everyone's attention? Uncle Roman acts as if he will be the next Grand Vampire.

CHAPTER THREE

The next morning, Elise followed the enforcers to the Cantonelli private airport hangar. Before Lucas and Santiago boarded the jet, Elise had a heart-to-heart talk with them and apologized for being so curt on the phone yesterday. They explained their worry was the only reason they had called, and it wasn't because they feared she'd fail to get the job done. When she was attacked and they'd seen her almost turned to dust, they realized that although immortal, a malicious attack such as beheading was the proven way to terminate a vampire's existence. Of course, they'd heard of it happening from time to time, however never so close to home. They had worked for Roman for over a hundred years and come to know all of the Cantonelli's. Although not blood related, the love and respect for one another was mutual. They would turn to dust for each other if it came down to it.

Focused on the task at hand, the men boarded the jet and waved bye to Elise from the small window. She waited until the jet was gaining altitude in the clear blue sky before she returned to her vehicle. Placing her sunglasses on her face, she started the engine and turned up the music before leaving the airport runway. *Now to prepare for her task...babysitting Grant.*

****

Grant awoke from his slumber and screamed for the purple-eyed captor. Where had she taken him? He sat up, realizing he was in a hospital bed wearing a red silk night shirt that went to his ankles. His hands and feet were bound to long chains that were attached to an iron ring fastened in the middle of the tile floor. The room was of an oval shape with the makeshift hospital room in the middle and a luxurious living room décor around it. Clearly, this was not a real hospital and he was not here voluntarily. His mind raced for answers as he looked around the room for clues. If only he could remember what happened. He relaxed his body against the pillows behind him as he tried to think why someone would abduct him. Was it for money?

Peering around the extended part of the room, he noticed the walls were painted an olive green and were hung with black and white framed photos. He was pretty far away from them and yet he could see every detail as if he was standing up close. His extreme perfect vision seemed odd to him. Trapped behind the glass frames were aerial views of a massive mansion surrounded by land and gated fences. He thought he even saw a massive cemetery with exquisite tombstones. Each photo was a different aerial view, and he couldn't help but think of how much money it must have cost to have them taken. Directly across from him was a fireplace with an elegant mantelpiece that must have been imported from Europe. Wherever he was, these people had exotic taste and must have a fortune. He must be in a cancer therapy clinic for lucrative business owners. That is the only reason he could come up with. But why were the chains necessary?

"I can assure you that this is not a cancer therapy clinic, Mr. Biltmore. The photos you are admiring were taken the first day I flew over the estate. I remember as if it was yesterday, as the crisp cool air brushed my face. It literally would have taken my breath away so I paid the current owner twice of what it was worth and moved in the same day," Roman said as he strolled up to the hospital bed.

He had heard every thought in Grant's mind and was trying to predict how the day would turn out once Grant knew the truth. He was hoping Grant would choose the vampire family, as he could tell Grant would be a valuable member. He hated to perform relinquishing on anyone. He also preferred to handle "newbies" himself so the history of their vampire history was told accurately and there were no safety issues for his personnel.

Grant had not heard a door open or footsteps alerting him that someone was in the room and the sudden voice startled him. His eyes widened in shock as he saw the man now standing at the foot of his bed. How did he know what Grant was thinking as he was certain he had not voiced his thoughts out loud? What was with this cape he is wearing? Suddenly he realized, he must be in a mental hospital.

Roman belted out in deep laughter as he tried to compose himself. "Mental hospital? That's a good one. I haven't heard that one yet." He took the chair next to the bed and crossed his legs and arms watching Grant intently. He could feel the twinge at his temples as he read Grant's thoughts and was very amused with his intellectual reasoning of this situation.

"I did not say anything. What are you talking about?" Grant asked, hoping for explanation. Roman ignored his question. The two men stared at each other until Roman finally broke the silence.

"Let's remove the restraints, shall we?" Roman said as he began to unbuckle the chained cuffs. He could have released them with just a wave of his hand, but it was too soon for Grant to see his powers. Trusting Grant would not try anything stupid, he turned his back to him, walked toward the fireplace, and placed a hand on the mantle to lean against it.

"Let's start with introductions, shall we? Obviously I already know your name. My name is Roman Cantonelli, the owner of this estate," he said proudly as he glanced toward the framed photos.

"I'm not sure that I want to know, but how do you know me?" Grant asked.

"I know you have a lot of questions and if you let me explain everything before you ask anymore, it will save us both a lot of time," he replied curtly.

Grant, shocked at his bluntness, nodded for him to proceed. So far, Roman thought he was handling his abduction and entrapment well. Anticipating the worst reaction Grant would express, he had an enforcer stationed outside the door in case things got complicated. If Roman was in need of assistance, a quick telepathic message would send the enforcer barging in. His trusted friend Bartholomew had worked for him going on fifty years and he was a most trusted employee. He was once a bodybuilder in Detroit and had the trophies to prove it. His clothes were specially ordered to fit around his tree trunk arms and the women craved his chiseled bulkiness. Roman remembered stumbling upon a badly bleeding man in an alley one night when hunting for prey. Turns out he was shot multiple times just for being African American. Roman quickly read his thoughts and memories only to be overcome with respect for how he coped with racism since the day he was born. His life was quickly fading and Roman made a choice to save him by biting his neck offering immortality. Roman then ordered enforcers to track down the men who shot him, wipe their memories as punishment, and banished them to a desert to suffer until they walked endlessly to their death. Bartholomew became like a son to him and was taught the history of vampires along with how to survive for the many years to come.

"Mr. Biltmore, I have been tracking you for a total of seven months now and am very impressed with the success of your business.

I also understand that you had a terminal illness that you had been dealing with on your own by hiding it from your employees and the few friends that you had," Roman announced and waited patiently for his reaction.

Grant bowed his head in defeat as he realized his illness was no longer a secret. He had worked so hard at keeping it from everyone so his business would continue to thrive and to avoid people's pity for him. However he didn't realize the mental toll it had on him, trying to disguise the pain and sickness he felt after every treatment. Every day, he had driven his expensive car and worn expensive suits with a phony smile on his face, all while his soul was slowly slipping from his body. He had tried everything to get rid of the cancer - from herbal supplements, awful-tasting drinks he had purchased off the internet, and by going to church every Sunday night to pray. When the clinical study became available, his doctor notified him and he signed up immediately.

Roman felt sorry for him as he listened to Grant's thoughts. The desperation he endured trying to stay alive had consumed him. Now he did not have to feel that anymore...as long as he agreed to the lifestyle.

"I'm sorry to interrupt, but did you say, had? Is my cancer in remission?" Grant asked with hope in his eyes.

"Mr. Biltmore you are a smart business-man and I will not beat around the bush. I am going to explain to you a story that will seem to be a fictional tale sold on shelves in book stores across the world. It is up to you to believe it and decide your destiny," Roman announced boldly.

This moment was pivotal to a newly-transformed vampire. How Roman told the tale would help determine the newbie's choice. Most newbies accepted the lifestyle they had been given but at times he'd had to relinquish those who could not accept what happened to them. Many potential vampire family members were turned to dust after refusing the lifestyle then threatening to tell their centuries long secret.

"I pitch a lot of proposals that seem rational to clients in hopes they buy my vehicles so I will try to understand yours," Grant said wearily.

Roman smiled and knew there was a reason he liked this guy. His rational thinking yet open-minded approach made him think that Grant's decision would be an easy one. He sat down in the red high-backed Victorian chair near the fireplace and began to disclose the history of vampire.

"A long time ago, a new civilization of people were born that were not quite like the rest. It is unsure how they were created however their existence were true. Knowing they were unlike the rest, they hid unnoticed in clusters all over Europe for many years until their population grew so large they had to spread out and acquire new living locations. This became a problem, due to their lifestyle of eating, socialization, and nocturnal preferences," Roman explained.

He paused to give Grant time to absorb the thought that a different culture of people besides humans existed. Seeing Grant look up at the ceiling trying to envision how these people may have looked, lived, and moved gave Roman the ok to continue further.

"These people were born with supernatural powers. Occasionally, a nosey mortal neighbor would witness their abnormal lifestyle and would run to their friend and spread rumors that humans were not the only ones living on earth. The secret was getting very hard to keep hidden and as more and more mortals were realizing the mystery people existed, it created hysteria. Of course, the mortals had to be dealt with to prevent any more trouble and orders were given to wipe their memories. Not all mortals could be found, which left the occasional mortal who knew the truth but the public deemed them insane."

Grant's eyes widened when he heard the words *supernatural* and *mortal*. His forehead scrunched and his eyes squinted as he leaned his head to the right, staring at the man sitting before him, trying to understand what was happening. He began to feel very uncomfortable around Roman and worried his memory would be wiped like the others. Sensing Grant's sudden resistance, Roman sat up straighter, on guard, in case he tried to flee.

"Mr. Biltmore, please try to listen to the whole story before drawing inaccurate conclusions," Roman demanded.

While dealing with Grant, Roman received a message from Elise stating she had returned and was waiting for his next command.

Everything was falling into place wonderfully and now he just had to convince Grant to become a part of the vampire family.

"The new civilization members were called immortals as they became aware that they never died, never became ill and if injured they healed at rapid speed. They did not breathe air or have a heartbeat as the mortals did. Their existence was obviously going to remain for many years to come and they had to adapt to the mortal world and maintain their lifestyle in secrecy. Every fifty years, an opportunity arose to where an immortal could choose a mortal to transform into their supernatural lifestyle that they saw could benefit their civilization," he slowly explained.

Grant was beginning to put the pieces together and instantly felt trapped. His eyes darted around the room in a panic while he thought of the men attacking him in the bathroom, the nightmares he had, his sudden healthy appearance and feeling, and finally the phone call he'd received from Dr. Rowland. How could this be happening? Bile rose in his throat and he placed his hand on his chest when he realized he was not taking or releasing air. He was not breathing! He quickly put two fingers on the inside of his wrist to check his pulse… and there was none.

Roman quickly stood up in preparation and then sent a message of "*Action is needed*" to Bartholomew at the door. It quickly swung open just as Grant leaped off the bed toward Roman. The enforcer reached for a syringe out of his pocket and jabbed it into Grant's thigh and held him, waiting for the effects to take hold. Moments later, Grant passed out cold as his body twitched in the enforcer's brute arms. Roman motioned for Grant's body to be placed back on the bed in restraints then began to leave the room, head bowed and disappointed.

"He didn't take it well, boss?" asked Bartholomew as he covered Grant's sleeping body.

Roman shook his head, disappointed, and went to his office for blood and to think of the next plan of action. Since being appointed the Grand Vampire fifty years ago, he'd had to make a lot of decisions that would affect his family and the other immortals of the world. It was a delicate yet admirable position to have and in ten years the next Grand Vampire would be called upon. Recently, the head of the Vampire Council had alerted Roman that they had found the next person to rule the vampire nation, however there was one problem, he was mortal. The Council was created hundreds of years ago and consisted of a six person panel of all retired Grand Vampires. They had a list of future immortal Grand Vampire prospects however, some had to be relinquished or they did not truly possess all the qualities needed for the position. As the Council researched Grant's background, they were informed of his terminal illness and the strides he made to continue living. Aware that there had never been a mortal chosen and turned specifically for the Grand Vampire position, they assumed Grant would be ever so pleased to continue life, but as an immortal and cancer free.

Roman sat at his desk, twirling the blood in a glass with his hand as he thought. He would do what he could to ease Grant's fears and help him accept his new lifestyle. In twenty-four hours, if he still resisted, he would notify the Council and he would have to relinquish him to dust. If Grant accepted becoming a vampire, Roman would wait until he was ready to hear that he would be the next Grand Vampire. Looking at the clock, he expected that when Grant woke he would be ready for his first feed. The thirst for blood would overcome his body, cause temporary blindness and inflict unbearable pain to his stomach which was really starvation of the body. Until he learned to hunt, he would have to drink blood from a glass.

It would be then, with that first taste of blood that his eyes would transform from his human color to beautiful purple eyes. Every vampire in the world had purple eyes, which would glow when they performed mind control or their senses heightened during love making. It was said by the elder vampire that when blood touched lips of newbies for the first time, it was the body's way of bidding farewell to the human life and a celebration of seeing life in a new perspective.

However, if an infant was conceived from immortal parents, the infant would also be born a vampire, and would already possess the breathtaking purple hue.

As Roman thought about the absence of children at his estate, he calculated that it had been at least one hundred years since a baby was born in their family. As the clock rang when it struck midnight,

Roman already deep in thought, received a premonition. He smiled as he drank the remaining contents of his dinner and thought soon the estate would once again echo with the pitter patter of tiny feet and laughter.

Chapter Four

It was just after two in the morning and Elise suspected the enforcers were busy with work in the west wing of the estate. She really didn't feel like working and decided she would mosey upstairs for a nice hot bubble bath. She climbed the stairs to her room when she remembered Grant was still on site. Turning on her heels, she retreated down the steps and into the elevator to the hospital level where Grant was being held. She would check on him quickly and then have her spa time.

Stepping off the elevator, she was greeted by Bartholomew.

"How's our newbie, Bart?" she asked.

He was reading the newest issue of, *Pump Power*, the local magazine for power lifters. It gave nutrition advice, recipes for power shakes, and tips on getting your ultimate muscle achievement. He would never have to worry about physical fitness again since becoming a vampire, but he still liked to maintain the routine and weight lifting discipline he practiced in his mortal life.

"He's been tossing and turning a lot, even after that shot I had to give him," he said.

Oh no, that meant he didn't take the news well. She wished her Uncle would have sent a message when she returned to the estate to subdue him with the sleep charm instead of reverting to the shot. On the other hand, she didn't know the guy, so why did she care?

"I'm going to go in and check on him. I'll alert you if there is trouble," she said to Bart.

He nodded and returned to his magazine.

She opened the door. The room was pitch black, but with the incredible eyesight immortals have, she could see as if every light was on. Noticing the fire was out in the fireplace, she wondered if it had given him comfort for it to be on. She walked over and turned the knob on the gas fireplace and set the timer for an hour. Watching the flames was soothing, and she recalled how comfortable it made her feel when she was turned a year ago. Those memories made her feel sorry for Grant, who was just going through what she had conquered. Never in her life would she want to go through that again.

Grant stirred in his bed, knocking off the sheet that covered his midsection. She picked it up off the floor and covered him back up and just sat at the edge of his bed. Staring at him as he slept, she couldn't help but think of how strong of man he was to try and battle cancer on his own without the support of family and friends. Now he didn't have to worry about dying, as long as he was ok with being a vampire. Their situations were the same, regarding being turned against their will. However, for some reason he was especially chosen. She was just in the wrong place at the wrong time when she was turned. *Why was he chosen to be turned?*

Elise wondered if he could sense her presence. She boldly grabbed his hand to see if he would budge. If he woke up in hysteria, she would just use mind control to calm him. She noticed his hands were big and fingers long, yet they looked manly with manicured nails. She laughed out loud then quickly covered her mouth as she thought about a man getting his nails manicured. He certainly was a man of wealth and was concerned about making sure people knew it. But why did looks matter so much to him?

Her temples began to twinge. Grant unexpectedly gripped her hand, then opened his honey-colored eyes and watched her as he lay motionless. Her attraction to him became overpowering. She looked back at him, startled and somewhat creeped out a little bit but she decided to try and talk to him.

"Hello, Grant. It's Elise, remember me?" she asked quietly.

He blinked his eyes and slowly rose up in bed. "I do. You abducted me and put me in a tricked-out vehicle," he said with his speech slurred.

Preparing to give him mind control if a problem arose, she asked him if he remembered anything from earlier. He nodded, "Why was that man wearing a cape?"

Elise belted out a hearty laugh as she had wondered that all of her childhood. She was still sitting at the side of his bed, holding his hand. Maybe babysitting Grant wouldn't be so bad after all. Just then a telepathic message came to her from Bart, telling her she only had a couple more minutes left to visit. She returned a message of *Thanks for the warning warden.*

"Listen, I know you've had a rough day so I will visit you tomorrow. If you need anything, let Bart know at the door," she said, and then realized he had already fallen back asleep.

****

Roman dialed the office of Crimson Records and selected option one to be directly transferred to Talion Masters, Recording Producer and Client Agent. Roman listened to the third ring and was preparing to leave a message when the line was answered.

"Crimson Records. This is Talion,"

"Talion, this is Roman Cantonelli. Do you have a moment?" Roman questioned.

"Certainly. What can I do for you?" he asked.

"We have an unexpected family matter that will take up most of Elise's time. She was telling me about her busy recording schedule in the next few months and I'm calling to tell you she will be unavailable," Roman boldly announced.

"What do you mean unavailable? She is under contract and required to release a new cd of at least twelve songs within thirty-two days. Failure to comply could result in her being released from Crimson Records and fined three million dollars. I'm not sure if you are aware Mr. Cantonelli, that the public craves more of Vanessa Rose. She needs to strike while the iron is hot and we've invested a lot of money if you get my drift," Talion explained desperately.

Roman was working hard to keep his temper under control while he listened to him whine. He then realized a visit in person would have probably worked out better if he brought along a female enforcer to persuade his acceptance of the situation. He remained calm by reminding himself his niece would not speak to him for eternity if he was the one responsible for ruining her music career.

"I assure you that I am aware of her contractual agreement and the fans love of...Elise. I mean, Vanessa Rose. I had an idea that I wanted to run by you. If you approve, I will begin construction today. I also believe that she had a private performance scheduled for the Countess of Corona. That will need to be rescheduled," Roman said with a smile, knowing Talion was cursing him out with the phone on mute.

"Excuse me? Rescheduled? Do you realize that the Countess is paying one million dollars for a sixty minute performance?" Talion shouted in a high-pitched voice.

"I expected you to react that way which is why I have a remedy that could help both of us," Roman concluded.

****

Lucas and Santiago returned from California the following morning. All was well at the blood supply warehouse and the employees received a bonus for the extra effort at concealing the family property. It turned out a couple of robbers had broken into the warehouse and saw the massive amount of blood stored as well as the Cantonelli family crest on each bag. The employees, were are also immortal, wiped the intruders' memory clean of the incident and sent them on their way home.

It was a close call, however it was the first slip up in sixty years - but it was handled rather fast and appropriately. Roman's employees feared him and would never leave room for error. Roman was pleased after receiving their update and was glad he had sent the enforcers to check on them. He had sensed something was just not right and once again his intuition was correct.

Roman had just sat down at his desk when Elise entered the room after waking up. She had planned on asking why Grant was chosen to be a vampire but got sidetracked when he confronted her on her visit with Grant last night. Nobody could keep anything away from him. His intuition was so powerful, she suspected that was one of the reasons why the Council had chosen him as Grand Vampire.

"How was Mr. Biltmore faring when you checked on him last night?" he asked with one eyebrow arched toward the sky.

Elise sat down on the brown leather sofa at the end of his desk knowing she had explaining to do.

"Bart said it would be okay to check on him. I just feel sorry for him…I guess," she said hesitantly.

Roman nodded his head to show he understood her mix of emotions. He just couldn't find the words to tell her he had visions that Grant would be her companion in the near future.

"Just to keep you informed I had a very long conversation with Talion. To keep it brief, I am building you a top of the line recording studio so you can work on your music and be here when I need you. My designer will be here this afternoon to create the blueprints. I have given her a week to complete it. The enforcers and gate patrol have been informed to engage the mortal visitor protocol," Roman quickly explained as he organized the file folders on his desk avoiding eye contact.

Elise was speechless and could not believe the extra work her Uncle was doing just to keep her at the estate to watch over Grant. There had to be more to the story but she did not want to show disrespect for his generosity by helping maintain her music career.

"Uncle, I am deeply grateful for your support. I will not let you down. What about the Countess? Did she agree to postpone the concert until all is well?" she asked.

"She did agree but with demands of her own only I can fulfill. Listen, I have to prepare for a meeting with the Council later. Will you be ok supervising our guest for a while?" he asked as he turned on the video screen mounted on the wall behind him. Due to the recent advances in technology, vampires used a global video and audio application called FangTime, to easily communicate and reduce traveling. Roman always made sure his fanged teeth were clean and his cape positioned dutifully before the Council would see him on video. He was actually very tired and couldn't wait to rest a spell.

Sometimes in emergency situations, Roman was interrupted during all times of the day and night. It took a while to program a vampire's body to maintain the sleep patterns of a mortal. Some could never learn to control the urge to sleep during the day and be awake and alert at night so each vampire had their own sleeping style. As a matter of fact, some newly immortals continued to sleep in their lush posture-pedic beds while older vampires burrowed in coffins to block light and for added protection.

Suddenly, the office door swung open startling the two of them.

"What is it, Bartholomew?" Roman asked, concerned.

"It is Mr. Biltmore. He is awake and alert, demanding answers. He does not seem well boss," Bartholomew announced.

Roman looked at Elise, silently giving her permission to resolve the situation.

"I'm on it," She whisked to the elevator with Bart at her heels.

****

Grant was dressed in a robe, sitting Indian style, on the floor, in front of the burning fireplace staring at the orange-tipped flames. He had awakened to memories of a caped crusader telling him about creatures with powers and then the moment of truth when he realized he was now one of those creatures. His stomach felt as if it was ripping apart and saliva flowed freely from his mouth. He had no clue what was happening and thought maybe they had poisoned him.

By the time Elise reached his room, he was curled up in a fetal position, moaning with his arms wrapped around his midsection and writhing in pain. She knelt beside him, realizing that his body was starving and he needed blood fast.

"Bartholomew, blood now!" she frantically yelled.

Grant looked back at her, unable to speak and silently pleading for help as he watched her purple eyes begin to glow. A wave of comfort enveloped his body and most of the pain receded. He felt instant relief as he watched her mind hard at work. He couldn't believe what he was seeing. It was amazing. Everything the caped man told him was true.

Bartholomew retrieved the crested blood supply bags like a bolt of lightning from the nearest walk-in refrigerator handing a blood bag to Elise. She reached for a bag then punctured a hole in it with her nail. The smell of blood filled the room enticing Grant enough that his new vampire fangs retreated from the top of his mouth instinctively. He felt his mouth painfully transform into a predator.

"NO!" he yelled in terror while holding his mouth.

Elise quickly demanded him to drink, as it was the only way to get rid of the pain. Without his acceptance, she secured the blood bag firmly to his newly-formed fangs and watched as they automatically siphoned the blood into his body. Slowly he began to feel ease as the knots in his stomach began to subside. To his surprise, the blood tasted amazing like a high-grade steak or his famous Sky Chili. He enjoyed it so much the bag was empty in minutes and Bartholomew plucked it from his fangs and immediately replaced it with a new bag.

"That's it, just drink now and all of the pain will go away. I realize how traumatic it is to be feeding from human blood but this is who you are now," Elise tried to explain soothingly.

Grant's eyes widened at her announcement that he was drinking a person's blood and he quickly looked at Bartholomew, with the bag barricading his mouth. Surely she was mistaken with her words. Bartholomew read his mind and replied with a telepathic message. *This is your new life now. I know what you are feeling and I promise to help you adjust.*

He had gone through his second bag and was feeling rejuvenated, however he craved more. Elise took the empty bag and then placed a third one on his fangs. Soon his once honey-colored eyes would turn to purple just like theirs. It was the body's way of adjusting to immortality.

As they all sat on the floor, Grant noticed his eye sight begin to fade until he only saw darkness. Then within seconds it reappeared and a glow immersed his eye sockets. There was no pain, only a tingling sensation, and then as soon as it started it went away. He opened his eyes and looked at Elise then Bartholomew and saw a wonderful grin painted on their faces.

"The transformation is now complete, Mr. Biltmore," she said lowering the empty bag from his mouth.

"Welcome to the family, brother," Bartholomew said with a caring smile.

Chapter Five

"So, you mean to tell me that you people changed me into a vampire to cure me from cancer?" Grant asked confused as he sat on the edge of his hospital bed.

Bart and Elise had felt it best for him to rest in bed. He wouldn't realize it yet, but his body conjured up all the energy to stay conscious while his body starved for blood. For the next few hours, he would have to consume more bags of blood than a normal vampire to replenish the energy lost during his hunger episode.

Bart and Elise sat near his bed as they explained to him again in detail about the lifestyle of a vampire and how they are not just in the comics. In fact, there were hundreds of thousands of vampires that walked the Earth each day but remained hidden from plain sight in order to protect their existence. There were good vampires, as well as bad vampires called Rogues. He needed to be able to tell the difference quick or he would not survive long.

"Mr. Biltmore, we are not sure why my uncle chose you to become a member of our family. I'm afraid that is only something he can answer. What you should focus on now is embracing what is in front of you, a chance of a long and healthy life," Elise said, rubbing the top of his hand.

Grant was still confused about the situation however he was smart enough to realize Elise had just flirted with him. Maybe eternity wasn't bad after all, if he could look at her beautiful face the whole time. In the back of his mind, he was a business-man and knew that this new lease on life would come with a price. There was no way he had been given the gift of immortality just out of the goodness of Roman's heart. If he had one, still. He sighed heavily as he realized that things would never be the same and he had a lot of questions.

****

Later that day, Elise briefed Roman on everything that had happened and watched as his expression never changed. She couldn't tell if he was pleased or not but you would think he would be ecstatic Grant was cooperating.

To change the subject, she explained to Roman that the designer was in and out within two hours with a finalized design and was informing the construction workers of the tight timelines that were given. Elise could tell the designer was not pleased about the rushed job but was paid very well for a quick and precise sound recording studio.

"Good work Elise," he praised.

Elise knew that was her cue to leave so Roman could assess Grant's mind. Her Uncle would soon find out if Grant would accept his new lifestyle or refuse and be relinquished. Of course, Roman had a feeling what the outcome would be.

Bartholomew please bring Mr. Biltmore to my office, Roman telepathically ordered.

Within minutes, Bartholomew knocked on the office door requesting entry with Grant. Roman opened the door with a wave of his hand without physically getting up from his office chair just to see how Grant would react.

Grant couldn't believe he'd just seen supernatural powers in real life but held his excitement to avoid risk of embarrassment. He was almost idolizing these people and he had just met them.

Roman grinned and extended a hand toward the open chair in front of him. Grant sat down and was busy exploring the various items hung on the walls. Bartholomew left the room and closed the door only to be stationed in the hallway in case he was needed.

"I hope my niece has been accommodating to your needs during this confusing time. Mr. Biltmore, this is a pivotal moment in which you must decide your fate. I will explain to you the circumstances before you ask any questions please," Roman stated.

"Yes, sir." Grant replied nervously.

"I trust you remember our conversation in your hospital room about how our kind came into existence and that we possess some pretty amazing powers," he continued.

Grant nodded. He would definitely ask his questions later, as he felt intimidated by this obvious authoritative man.

"The Vampire Council has been watching you for quite some time and became intrigued with you. Your savvy business skills and professional work ethic is hard to find among mortals these days. The success of your automobile business is something to be proud of," he boasted as he sifted through Grant's business financial records.

Grant was surprised he was getting a compliment from a person who possessed his own worldly powers. He felt he was nothing compared to the things the man before him could do in one lifetime.

"We also know that you suffered from an illness doomed to be fatal. Your close companions and employees were unaware for months as you maintained your daily routine without a flaw and remained positive. That shows a lot from a man and you have refreshed our thoughts of the human race today. The overall positivity mortals lack in this century is pathetic," Roman said, as he stared at the purple eyed newbie.

Centuries. How old was this man?

"I am 470 years old, Mr. Biltmore," Roman replied with his hands folded on his desk.

Roman gave Grant a moment to digest what he had just revealed to him. He felt Grant's admiration for him increase since he first set foot in his office. Roman was now certain that he would accept his fate as a vampire and would join the Cantonelli family.

"Mr. Biltmore, let me be clear. You were chosen not by me, but by the Vampire Council in Italy to become a member of the immortal family because of the value you could be to us. You may not understand now, but this is a high honor and something to be proud of. Not to mention their choice saved you from a horrible disease that was killing you from the inside. There are a few things you must realize before confirming your decision. One, you are dead. You have no pulse; you longer need air to breathe. That night at the chili parlor, my men took your life and traded it with immortality. Two, the nightmares you endured were memories of the turn and your healthy glow and cancer remission the next day was a result of your new gift. I'm a very blunt man, Mr. Biltmore, if you haven't noticed. Your human-self died that night and you have been reborn a vampire."

There was a knock at the door and Bartholomew allowed Lucas and Santiago to step in.

"You may remember these faces from that night," Roman said.

Grant stood up and met the gaze of the vampires who'd bit him. They stood in all-black attire with arms folded as if on guard from an apocalypse.

"You bit me?" Grant asked in denial.

"Forgive me for not offering proper introductions. Grant, these are the enforcers I tasked with your turn, Lucas and Santiago Ortega. They are brothers and work for me as enforcers against Rogue vampires."

"No way! The Ortega brothers are vampire?" he asked in disbelief.

Lucas and Santiago chuckled at his reaction of meeting them. It was rare that someone remembered who they were and felt like celebrities when it did happen. They were famous baseball players who had played for the Cobra's many years ago. Their death was a shock to all of the US as it was stated in the media that they perished in a bus accident on their way to a game.

"Sorry about the bite, man. Boss' orders." Lucas said as he shook Grant's hand.

"Yeah, you seemed like a nice guy and we felt bad for deceiving you like that. We don't like to hurt our fans," Santiago said, trying to lighten up the situation.

Roman understood the moment of awe, however business came first. He glared at all three men, wishing they would control themselves. Immediately Lucas and Santiago redeemed their composure and military-like stance.

Grant cleared his throat and sat back down in his chair like a reprimanded school boy. Thoughts were racing in his mind. What happens next? Would he be able to keep working or would he have to fake his death like the Ortega brothers?

"First matter of business is to discuss the requirements of being a vampire. We will have to arrange your human death so it appears you no longer exist. That means you will no longer associate with employees or friends who knew you in that life. You will need to move into the estate so you can be protected and trained as a vampire. Lastly, you will work for me under a contractual agreement at double the amount you are making now in exchange for part ownership of your auto business," Roman ordered all at once.

"How do you expect me to make all of these changes at once? This is unreasonable. I did not ask for this," Grant said as he felt a wave of emotions.

Roman ordered Lucas and Santiago to leave the room in a telepathic message. *Go to the hallway and wait for my next assignment.* Grant watched them leave and feared the worst was coming. This was it. He was toast.

"It has been a long time since I was turned so I tend to forget the inconvenience this may cause. My niece has a soft spot for newly turns as she was turned unexpectedly not too long ago. I believe she can assist you in processing the emotions the changes will cause and any other new feelings you may have," Roman explained, then paused for his last comment to sink in.

Grant was caught off guard and crossed his legs while eyeing the caped man. He was pretty sure that Roman sensed that he found his niece attractive. So, was this his approval for Grant to pursue her if he joined the family, he wondered?

"Regarding my orders of the next steps you must take, assuming you choose to join our family, remain non-negotiable. You must realize this is all necessary to protect your immortality and most importantly the whole vampire existence," he explained in a softer tone.

Grant stood up then paced the room back and forth, eventually stopping in front of a huge gold framed mirror. He stepped closer realizing he now had purple eyes just like the rest of the vampires. He blinked several times for proof they were real. He had not seen himself since he left his home the day before and was still astonished at how young, healthy, and vibrant he looked. His muscles were more toned and his hair no longer had gray hair sprouting at his temples. He touched his face as if he was an alien just discovered. He liked what he saw as tears began to form in the inner corners of his eyes.

He swiftly turned around toward Roman, "I'm in."

CHAPTER SIX

In the conference room Roman used FangTime with the Council informing them that the turn of the new family member was successful. They congratulated Roman for the great leadership he gave on this project and then announced they would be leaving Prague to visit in six months to meet Grant. It was a great honor to host the Vampire Council and the news would be exciting for the whole Cantonelli family. His persistence paid off, but now Roman would be expected to have Grant's human existence diminished formally, moved into the estate and trained fully as a vampire by then. He certainly had a lot of work to do.

The Council then revealed the next assignment to Roman. He would need to leave his family in ten years to become a member of the Vampire Council in Prague. They explained that there was nobody else suitable or more respected than Roman to be the head of the Vampire Council. Roman was stunned by the news as he was usually informed of such decisions through his premonitions and did not see this one coming. Was he lacking in his powers? The current head of Council, Creighton read his mind and admitted they suppressed the information from their minds prior to each meeting in order for it to be a special surprise.

He thanked them for the consideration and accepted the position admirably. Now he just needed to explain to Elise his reason for leaving but of course he had ten years to do so. He would not worry about that now. He bid farewell to the Council before adjourning their meeting and once the video screen went blank he sat in his office, staring at the walls. Roman wondered if the Vampire Council read his thoughts about the upcoming events for his family. Did he really want to leave his family knowing of the changes coming in Elise's life?

****

Elise and Grant retreated to the library on the third floor to begin lessons. The library was packed with books dating back to when immortality was first discovered to the most recent published. The old books had to be stored in specialized containers to preserve them from the pollutants and other factors that could damage them. The containers were electronically monitored for air, temperature, and lighting control. They had to be kept at room temperature or below and thirty five percent relative humidity with no exposure to intense or direct lighting. At no point were the books allowed to be handled or pages touched. For vampires, touching was not necessary as their powers allowed them to turn pages with a wave of their hand. A book could not leave the library unless it was an emergency. If a book was needed outside of the library, the book and the container would be checked out, never taking the book out of the container. The container was specially created of a special glass to refract light and avoid extensive light damage.

Elise skimmed through the pillars of books until she found the one titled, The First Thirst and carefully placed the container on one of the study tables. Her eyes glowed as she sifted through the pages by wave of her hand. Grant felt privileged just being in the same room with literature so old it classified as a museum item.

"I hope we look of this quality when we are this old," Grant said.

"OK, focus. The first thing we need to teach you is feeding. Usually, newbies are so freaked out about hunting that they first learn to drink from a glass or a blood bag. If you do not feed every couple of hours, you will feel that horrible pain again. You must carry bags on you in case of emergency if you will be out in public for long periods of time. Bartholomew chooses to wear a messenger bag but Lucas prefers a backpack. It is really dependent upon your fashion taste and what is easiest to maneuver during a fight if a Rogue attacks. I can't stress this next rule enough, but only drink from a blood bag with the family crest on it. We screen the blood thoroughly at our warehouse to make sure Rogue vampires did not put any charms on it. Trust me, you do not want to drink any charmed blood," Elise explained to Grant like a mother.

"I would never picture Bartholomew as one who would carry a messenger bag. I guess you and I will have to add purse shopping on our to-do list," Grant said, looking for an excuse for them to be alone.

Elise felt a wave of excitement that took her by surprise. The way he looked at her made her feel like a normal woman again. She had not had those feelings in a long time since her turn. Her body must have also sensed the new emotion as her cheeks began to blush and she became very nervous around him.

Grant noticed the alteration in her demeanor and realized he had just flirted with his immortality mentor. He needed to change the subject, quick.

"So, what are charms?" Grant asked, as he avoided eye contact.

"Charms are spells that Rogue vampires use as a silent weapon against us. Think of it as voodoo magic. They are powerful and can cause a lot of damage especially since it is not easily noticed when one is infected. Most charm infections are confirmed by witnessing actions and words that are out of the ordinary of your personality. It could go on for days or weeks depending on if the task of the charm has been completed," she revealed.

"Wow, this just gets even more complicated. So, in other words, it's like another form of mind control when the Rogues are not able to be in close proximity to their victim. I am going to write all of this information down to help me remember all of this. Can you explain more about hunting? I was not much of an outdoorsman in my prior life and camo was never my color of choice," Grant joked, trying to get his teacher to smile.

"I do not mean the sport of animal hunting, silly. Hunting mortals is how we feed and flourish. Vampires need mortal blood, plain and simple. It sounds callous and immoral but it has to be done. Most vampires choose to hunt, that way the blood is fresh. We usually only go out at night, however in an emergency we can hunt in daylight but you have to be extremely careful of sunlight and being gone too long. We will see how you are doing in a couple weeks and I might take you on a hunt. If you are a good boy," she said with a wink.

Grant was not impressed with becoming a blood-sucking monster who preyed on innocent people. He could never see himself doing that but then again he never expected to become something created out of a Hollywood set either.

"Please tell me I will not have to wear a cape like your uncle," Grant stated, horrified at the thought of wearing it in public.

"I assure you the cape is not mandatory. During the time of my uncle's birth as a vampire it was a customary accessory for immortals to wear," she confirmed.

"That is the best news I've heard so far today. So do you people eat food like spaghetti, pizza, or ice cream? I mean, do I totally have to abandon all of my mortal perks?" Grant asked, pleading like a child.

Elise laughed at his sense of humor and acknowledged that they could eat mortal food, however the thirst for blood exceeded the want for it. She could tell that Grant was becoming more relaxed and eager to learn his new lifestyle.

"OK, enough about food. The fun begins. Let's go plan your death!" Elise said, smiling as she sent a telepathic message to the enforcers of their next plan. This assignment of babysitting Grant was bringing some good memories back that she hadn't thought of in a while. She liked it. She liked him.

****

Elise drove Grant to his office as they rehearsed their plan. Lucas tagged along just for the fun of it. It was always entertainment for them to watch newbies put on a theatrical performance. Unlike actors, they had to play the part perfect in order for the audience to believe it was real. However, it can be emotional for the newbie because it is their final goodbye to anyone they formed a relationship with. To them, it was true death of a formal life and everyone that was in it.

As if reading a script, Grant practiced his lines while on the way to his business, "I am afraid to tell the fine people that I hold dear, I....am....dying."

"Yeah, um you aren't Clark Gable. I've met him. That is not convincing at all," Lucas said unamused.

"Sorry, I've never had to fake my own death before. This is a little stressful," Grant said, irritated.

"It's ok. I've got it under control." Elise slipped her shades on and cranked up the music.

Ironically, Aerosmith's *"Livin on the Edge"* came on and Lucas and Elise broke out into a duet and as they bobbed their heads up and down. Grant was not used to being around people who were so laid back and enjoyed music so much. Elise had a really nice voice and could have her own radio station if she wanted to. Grant would listen to her all day long. He stared at her, taking in her beauty that she did not realize she had. Her short hair was framed perfectly around her angelic face. She was tall enough to not need high heels but he could tell she always wore the same black boots. It fit her style, he guessed. He typically would not have thought her as his type in his mortal life. However, he saw life with a new set of eyes, literally.

When the song was over, she turned the radio down to focus on the road when she noticed Grant watching her. At first she thought he was hungry, fighting the urge to bite her but then read his mind and realized he was having romantic thoughts. *Holy crap, I'm falling for a newbie.*

"This stuff should be on a reality show," Lucas said, cracking up in the passenger seat.

"Shut up, Lucas," Elise said angrily.

Grant knew he was missing something between the two telepathically. He couldn't wait until he learned how to read minds, especially Elise's.

Finally, turning into the parking lot of XL Auto Company they rehearsed their plan for the fifteenth time, making sure everyone understood. Grant would make his announcement to the whole office and then privately pitch Roman's offer of buying the company with his business partner, Ethan. Elise shut the engine off and everyone exited the vehicle and walked toward Grant's personal side entrance to his office. With a swipe of Grant's employee badge to the access box positioned on the door frame, the red security light turned green, allowing access. To his surprise, everything in his office was as he left it and the lights were off, showing no signs of anyone using his office. Good. He did not like people rooting through his personal items. He sat down in his leather office chair and opened drawers to gather his belongings. He began to feel nervous as he was sure he would be asked a ton of questions about where he had been. A picture of the ribbon cutting on the day of when his business opened laid in the bottom of his drawer staring back at him. He would never forget the feeling of accomplishment and adrenaline that day. It somewhat made him feel like all the hard work was for nothing.

Elise watched him sift through the items in his drawer and read his mind as he looked at each photo, document, and sale sheet. She felt the pain as well as the pride he was experiencing and how he handled this situation made her respect him even more. He should not linger in this place much longer.

"OK, this is it. Are you sure you don't want me to just wipe their memory of you?" Elise asked feeling nervous for Grant.

"No, I need to do this myself for closure, if you don't mind," Grant said as he looked at both his vampire friends for approval. Elise and Lucas decided to hide in Grant's private bathroom with the door shut and light off to listen as he said goodbye to his employees. If at any time he needed their assistance they were just steps away.

****

Grant pressed the button on the speaker phone to summon Mona to his office. He decided to put the lighting on low so they wouldn't notice his healthy, young appearance, and purple eyes. He adjusted the setting with just enough light for the mortals to move around. Gradually, he started to see heads peering up over their cubicles to see if it was actually him. He grinned as he realized he would miss the nosey office people yearning for any kind of gossip to make the work days go faster. In a state of shock, Mona, his secretary, hung up her thirty-minute private call on the company dime and reapplied her lipstick as she fiddled for a notepad and pen in preparation of entering her boss' office.

"Mr. Biltmore, I am surprised to see you. I mean... everyone has been wondering where you have been. But don't worry; I told them you had an important meeting with potential new clients in.... Aspen," she said with a wink, as if she had his back.

Grant sensed she was staring at him like something wasn't right and he began to fidget with the papers lying on his desk. He hoped she didn't notice his new physical appearance. Just then he received a telepathic message from Elise, giving him words of encouragement. *You can do this!*

Grant tightened his tie at the base of his neck and prepared himself for the charade.

"This is going to sound like an odd request but would you gather everyone for me and bring them to my office for a meeting?" he asked, avoiding her elongated gaze.

Mona cleared her throat and put her right arm on her hip showing resistance with his request.

"You want me to round up all sixty-three employees to have a meeting in here? Your office is not large enough for all of the employees, sir. I will check to see if the conference room is available instead," she said, twirling around to walk out the door.

"Mona, no. I'm not feeling very well and I would like to remain in one spot if that's possible. Thank you."

She turned her head around with a perplexed look on her face but finally agreed. She personally walked to each cubicle and office informing them of an emergency meeting being held in Mr. Biltmore's office trying her best to avoid any questions from the staff.

Immediately people began to panic, thinking they were about to be laid off or the company was being merged with another company. They all began to whisper as they walked toward Grant's office though they tried to put on happy emotions upon entering. After a couple of minutes, Mona accounted for everyone and nodded to Grant as a sign to begin.

"Thank you, Mona, for gathering everyone for this special meeting. I understand the weekend is near and you are wishing to get home to your families. I called this meeting to announce some important news. I have been hiding something for months that can no longer be a secret and as part owner of the company I come to you today not as your boss or employer, but as your friend."

The men and women standing in his office began to look at each other in confusion and worry. He paused for a moment to let the words to sink in. Emotions came to him that he was not prepared for and he quickly wiped a tear forming in his eye. He understood he was a private person and kept mostly to himself so the sadness was not for having to say goodbye, but of his regret for not fully living when he had the chance.

On many occasions, he was invited to sports games, grill outs, and holiday parties from his employees but he had declined them all because he just simply did not want to go. But the irony is, he knew who each person was, marital status, how many children they had, and of course their salary. He appeared to many people as arrogant and detached from social interaction but deep down he just didn't feel he fit in. Although he was technically dead, he had a chance to relive life, just not as a mortal.

"The truth of the matter is … I'm dying. I've had an aggressive cancer for months and have tried many rounds of chemotherapy. I come to you today to bid you farewell. Under the advice from my doctors, I have been getting my final arrangements together and have been tidying up loose ends. I could go into more detail with you, but I simply do not have the energy. I wish you all a prosperous life and thank you for making this company a success. I will be selling my share of the company and I urge you to continue the hard work as you have been doing for years. I am confident that XL Auto has a bright and prosperous future. It has been a pleasure watching your families grow."

Some of the women had tears streaming down their faces, looking at Grant with such pity. The men hung their heads low, not knowing what to say. A few employees had no reaction and left the room in a hurry to avoid the difficult situation.

Mona, was the first person to speak by stepping forward, offering her condolences on behalf the whole department and stated he was a wonderful person to work for. As everyone left the office to return to their cubicles, Mona stayed behind and shut the door.

"Mr. Biltmore my heart aches for you and if there is anything I can do for you please let me know. You have been my employer for over thirteen years and I appreciate everything you have done for me. I value our close relationship and will remember you always,"

Mona said, as she produced fake tears and reached for a tissue out of her pocket.

Waiting quietly, Elise and Lucas heard Grant's speech and thought it was very moving. They had to fight back the tears forming in their purple eyes. At that moment, they both felt becoming a vampire was Grant's destiny.

As they listened to Mona speaking to Grant, Lucas decided to read Mona's thoughts and became startled and paced back and forth. Elise knew he was hiding something from her. She could have easily read Mona's mind for the answer but she knew that Lucas would spill the beans.

"What is it?" she asked.

"It appears Grant's secretary is trying to entice her employer into thinking she really cares for him. Truth of the matter is that she knows he is a single man, with no family and is wealthy. That dreadful woman is actually hoping he leaves her money or cars in his will," Lucas confessed, and was appalled.

Without thinking about the consequences Elise became enraged and opened the bathroom door with a wave of her hand, revealing their presence. She had to warn Grant.

Lucas knew there was no calming Elise down when she was angry so he let her rant continue. He followed right behind her, in case their "talk" got complicated. Since Mona was female, Lucas was the only trained male vampire in the room who could use mind control to subdue her if need be.

Adrenaline coursed through Grant as he saw his new family emerge from the shadows so abruptly while Mona was still in the room. *Did they not still hear her talking?* Bewildered, he glanced at Elise then Mona, then to Lucas in confusion. He thought he had things under control and did not understand why they were coming to his rescue already.

Elise walked up to Mona and pointed her index finger in her face, "You are the most disgraceful mortal I have ever met."

Grant immediately stood up, causing his office chair to hit the back wall and started to walk toward the women when Lucas intervened and told him to relax. Taking his advice, he remained standing behind his desk and watched Lucas grab Elise by her arm and slide her out of the way to face Mona.

Mona's face was frozen with fear as she looked at these people with their glowing purple eyes, wearing clothes out of *The Matrix*. Her mouth started to open to scream when Lucas stared deeply into her eyes to gain control of her mind. Within seconds, her mind and body were like a puppet and Lucas was holding the strings. He told her to sit down and that everything was fine and to relax.

"Yes, I will relax," Mona said in a monotone voice like a robot.

Realizing Mona was no longer a threat of revealing their secret Grant approached Elise hastily demanding an explanation of why she said those nasty words.

"You don't know what she was thinking!" Elise said with her teeth clenched.

Lucas watched them exchange glares and knew this situation was getting ugly fast. "Um, guys," he said as he stared at Mona with glowing eyes. He wasn't going to control her all day just because they were arguing. They were professional enforcers on a job that was getting out of hand. If Roman heard about this he would be furious.

"Oh, great. So just because you have these magical powers it gives you the right to use them on my secretary?" Grant asked angrily.

"She is not a good person and I assure you that she is not a nice mortal," Elise confidently said.

"Who are you to judge? If this is how your family operates then count me out. I have worked here for a long time and know these people very well and if you think for a second..."

"She is being nice to you for one reason Grant, in hopes to inherit your money when you pass!" Elise blurted out unexpectedly. She raised her hand to her mouth as she realized she had not told him in the most pleasant way. His feelings were hurt, and she could see the disappointment on his face.

Grant looked at Lucas for validation but Lucas was focused on Mona. His gut felt that Elise was telling the truth but it was incomprehensible. *How could his secretary be so conniving?* He turned on his heels and bolted out his side office door.

"I'm going after him," Elise said.

"What do you want me to do with her?" Lucas asked.

Elise looked at Mona, ready to choke her out for causing a rift between her and Grant. But then she realized she needed to get her emotions in check. *Why did she care so much about what Grant thought of her?*

"Erase her memory of us ever being here. I don't care what you plug in her mind, just be quick before anyone comes in," Elise said as she ran out the side door after Grant.

CHAPTER SEVEN

The car ride back to the estate was eerily quiet as the friction between Grant and Elise grew. Elise was so tense in the driver's seat that she didn't even turn the radio on. Grant stared out the passenger side window, watching the silver guard rail on the interstate move with the car. Lucas chose to sit in back to avoid the feud. He could not believe that Elise had given up their position just to warn Grant of Mona's devious plan. It could have backfired and most importantly the other employees may have seen the altercation. Lucas smiled as he realized the real problem of the situation. He shook his head, looking at Elise in the rear-view mirror.

"You have feelings for Grant, don't you?" Lucas said to Elise telepathically.

Elise jerked the steering wheel to the right, surprised at Lucas' question and everyone's body jerked with the motion of the car. Grant turned his head to look at her to see if she was okay.

"Sorry there was a possum in the middle of the lane," Elise lied defiantly while glaring at Lucas through the mirror.

To change the subject, Elise asked Lucas how he handled the woman and if anyone had seen them. She had to fill in Uncle Roman about the assignment when they returned, and she needed to have her facts straight.

"Oh. I erased her memories of seeing us but made sure she remembered Grant's speech. I placed in her mind that she then saw a mouse run across the floor. Right now she's probably still standing on top of Grant's desk screaming and flailing her arms. Then I slipped out the side door," he said as he laughed.

All three of them laughed and smiled as they were picturing Mona in hysterics while other people were trying to calm her down. The notion was devious but at least Grant knew that vampires had a good sense of humor. It seemed to help lighten the mood which eased the tension just in time as they approached the entrance of the estate.

As they pulled up the cobblestone circle driveway to the main entrance, they saw a moving van parked out front. There were many workers going in and out of the vehicle and into the mansion. Looking at some of the furniture, Grant realized it was all of his belongings from his condo.

"What are my things doing here? I told Roman that I would make arrangements to move by the end of the week," Grant asked, perplexed.

"One thing you have to learn around here is that Roman does everything when it's good for him. You were taking too long," Lucas said as he patted Grant's shoulder and exited the vehicle.

Grant looked at Elise in disbelief of Roman's lack of patience.

She smiled, then shrugged and said, "Welcome home."

****

"So you mean to tell me that you revealed your position because you did not like the thoughts of the secretary?" Roman asked with his brow arched while tapping his fingers on his desk in annoyance.

Bartholomew, Lucas, Santiago, and Elise were having their debriefing like they normally had after every assignment. Elise poured a hefty glass of chilled blood and sat on the couch, waiting for the lecture. Ashamed and lowering her head, she nodded her head yes waiting for her Uncle's disappointment. Lucas and Santiago sat on the opposite end of the couch while Roman sat in the middle of the room in his high-backed chair as always.

"But, Uncle, that woman knew Grant has a fortune and no kin to give it to. She was going to use Grant's illness as a way to get closer to him in hopes he would leave it to her," Elise voiced her displeasure strongly.

"I see. So Grant now knows what her true intentions were?" Roman asked.

"For the record sir, I erased all memories of us and took care of the situation. I do not see her being a potential threat to the immortal family," Lucas said, hoping to ease Elise's worry.

"Not all of the assignment was completed. He did not meet with his business partner before the chaos erupted. I will be stepping out for a bit to finish the assignment. Santiago, you will see that Grant's belongings get put away and he is settled comfortably in the house. Elise, you may take the rest of the day off. Bartholomew can cover your shift," Roman announced as he rose from his chair, signaling the meeting was over.

Roman quickly walked out of the room and out the front door, leaving the enforcers standing in the office. They were unhappy about the mission being unfinished but more importantly shocked that Roman was personally taking it over.

****

The moving men had placed all of Grant's belongings in a spacious suite located on the second floor. He couldn't believe that the mansion was so big that it required elevators according to state law. He counted the floor level buttons on the elevator, six including the ground floor. This was like a small city and it would take some getting used to. All of his clothes were on hangers in boxes so that all he had to do was open the box and place them in the closets. The items were left in the drawers of his furniture and just and just taped shut so nothing fell out. Roman certainly coordinated things perfectly and in a speedy fashion. He assumed it wasn't the first time he had to quickly move a new vampire into his home. His mind wondered how many people Roman turned into vampires as he put away his belongings and arranged furniture around the suite.

"Twenty-three to be exact," Santiago said as he stood in Grant's doorway.

Grant had to remember that his thoughts were no longer private and would have to learn how to guard them around other immortals.

"You will soon learn how to do that, too. Also, you will learn how to send and receive telepathic messages." Santiago said smiling as he leaned in the doorway, eating an apple.

Grant chuckled at Santiago's bold personality. He could tell they would become great friends. Grant began to move the queen sized, pillow-top mattress and box spring onto the bed rails, and realized they were not heavy at all. Normally, it was necessary to have two people balancing the weight.

"Immortals possess powerful strength in order to protect themselves from Rogues or mortals who are trying to kill them. Soon your muscles will develop into canons like mine," Santiago explained humorously as he flexed an arm curl.

Grant lowered the top mattress onto the box spring and started not to feel well. He tried to think of what it could be when Santiago asked him when he fed last. Feeling like an idiot, Grant realized his body craved blood. He had not fed in a while and this would be a routine he definitely needed to keep track of.

"Let's go get you a refrigerator stocked with blood to keep in your suite. I can also answer any other questions you may have," Santiago said.

****

Santiago and Grant enjoyed a couple glasses of blood together in the enormous rustic, yet contemporary decorated kitchen. They spoke of experiences that happened in their mortal life and were bonding nicely. Grant thought Santiago was an easy person to speak too and felt comfortable asking the obvious questions a new vampire would have.

"Santiago, what exactly is a Rogue vampire?" Grant asked.

"A Rogue is a loner vampire who carries out devious acts on mortals. They believe that it is okay to feed on them until they drain every drop of blood, killing them instantly. They cover the bite marks and flee the scene, leaving a family in pieces because they think it is fun. I despise them, and that is why I became an enforcer," Santiago replied, twirling his glass to watch the blood move.

"But Elise said that I will be hunting. How will I know when I've taken too much blood? I can't believe I am even having this conversation. Maybe I will just stick to drinking blood from a bag or glass," Grant said feeling unsure.

"That is an option; however you need to learn how to hunt in case there are times when a bag of blood is not available. If you are out in the city and cannot make it back to the estate before the pains begin you will have to feed on the spot," Santiago explained.

Grant nodded. He understood that not being near a source of blood could cause death to a vampire.

Grant was going to ask questions about Elise so he could try and understand her personality when she walked into the room rummaging through cabinets, looking for a mug to make coffee. She was in a robe after just taking a shower and she didn't say a word to the men as she turned the coffee pot on and stood there with her back toward them.

"I'm going to check in on Roman and see how the assignment is going," Santiago said abruptly as he patted Grant on the shoulder and left the kitchen.

Elise took Santiago's chair and prepared for her coffee by getting the creamer and sugar ready without looking at Grant. She didn't know what to say to him after the altercation at his office. She knew that his feelings were hurt but she was just looking out for him when she confronted Mona. To be honest, the way she reacted was a little out of character. She supposed she owed him an apology as well.

Sensing the friction, Grant decided to break the ice, "I'm sorry that I reacted the way I did back at the office. I just was shocked to hear that someone would have the nerve to deceive me like that;

especially when it was one of my trusted employees," Grant explained, truthfully.

The coffee was now filled to the brim of the pot and Elise stood up and walked over to the counter to pour it into her mug. Grant watched her as he waited for a reply. Surely she was not going to ignore him. He watched her stand there, slowly pouring the brew, and began to think about how quickly his life had changed in the last few days. It certainly was different and full of future possibilities. He wondered if Elise was one of those possibilities. Actually, he hoped.

Elise straightened her back as she felt his gaze and heard his last thought. Could it be true that Grant was beginning to have feelings for her, too? She was not going to rush into things, after all she had just met him and he still had to learn the ropes of immortality. But, Uncle Roman did give Grant to her as an assignment, therefore being around him was not a personal choice. It was indeed, unprofessional to refuse a mission.

With a subtle smile, she reached in the drawer for a spoon and sat back down, looking Grant in the eyes. She wanted to test if his telepathic abilities were beginning to form and wondered if he would allow her to see.

"I accept your apology, and I am also sorry for almost ruining the whole assignment. I don't know what got into me but when I knew that she was deceiving you I wanted to strangle her. I would only hope that if I was in the same situation, someone would warn me of disloyal friends," she said.

Elise poured in the creamer and sugar then used her spoon to slowly stir the contents. Silence filled the room, since they didn't know what else to say to each other. Moments later, almost as if Grant was reading her mind, he asked if he could try to send her a message telepathically.

Intrigued at his willingness to learn, she happily agreed and watched him try different ways to relay the message. He would squint his eyes as he stared at the top of her head. When that didn't work he held one eye open as he closed the other. After several humorous attempts, she offered some gentle advice.

"Relax your body and clear your mind, leaving only the message you wish to relay. Focus on each letter in the word then silently say my name. If I receive it, I will respond the same way. Let's start with just one word," she said soothingly.

Grant closed his eyes and placed his hands in his lap. He wanted to experience this so bad and would try all night if he had to. He concentrated on emptying his thoughts from his mind and a moment later he finally could see each letter of the word he wanted to relay. Afraid it would disappear, he quickly said Elise's name in his mind and sent the message then immediately opened his eyes for acceptance.

Elise couldn't believe how smoothly the newbie was adapting to the vampire lifestyle. She sat a moment bewildered at the rate he was learning and understood why the Council had chosen him to be a vampire. Grant was very antsy in his seat, like a child waiting to be called on by the teacher as he anticipated her to say something. He studied her face for a hint and realized she was now looking at him differently.

"You said the word Haven if I'm not mistaken." Elise said. Grant shouted out a "yes" and raised his arm into air performing a fist pump. Elise laughed excitedly as she remembered how she felt when she relayed her first telepathic word to Santiago. Her first telepathic word was music. It truly is an amazing feeling.

"OK, hot shot. Finish your whole message now." Elise said challenging him.

Grant nodded then relaxed his body and cleared his mind without the need to close his eyes this time. He wanted to see her reaction to every word that she received. His gaze was even more serious this time which lured Elise closer anticipating what he had to say. The longer the eye control he held with her the more his eyes began to glow. She began to feel the same energy she had felt before as if her chest was going to explode and grabbed the side of the table with her right hand for control. Grant must have felt it too because his left hand quickly rested on top of her hand tightening the grip. He finally released his message saying *"Your eyes are my purple haven."*

The words struck her like a lightning bolt and her hands began to sweat then shake. Not realizing she was still gripping the table and that Grant's hand was on top of hers she stood up not knowing what to do. Grant helped her stand while holding her hand until she gained her composure.

"I assume you received my message?" Grant asked as he looked into her eyes. The glow he had during the session was gone but his eyes were fixated on hers in an endearing way she was not quite used to. She wasn't exactly thrilled that a newbie was interested in her romantically but this handsome man standing in front of her was exactly what she needed in her life. Since her own turn, she had not been with a man and she was embarrassed to admit her nervousness.

Elise was sure her cheeks were flushed as she felt the warmth radiating from her skin. She hadn't smiled like that in a long time and felt like a teenager again. Her smile quickly faded as she noticed his face turn pale and then almost gray. His legs became wobbly until he fell over and began to lose consciousness. He wasn't sure what was happening but he knew it wasn't good. The last thing he remembered was her yelling for Santiago while she caressed his forehead with her palm for comfort.

CHAPTER EIGHT

Grant awoke to a pitch black room, soon realizing he was lying in his own bed comfortably. He didn't remember returning to his room a couple hours earlier but he did have a slight headache and a huge appetite. He sat up in his bed looking around his room remembering his moment with Elise when he found her slumped in a plush lounge chair next to his bed sleeping. He needed to grab some blood and use the restroom but didn't want to wake her so he quietly pulled back the cover and gently rose from bed. He watched her face looking for signs of waking and took in the beauty of her beautiful cherub face. He knew they had a connection and knew that she felt it too. A throw blanket rested at the foot of his bed and he gently retrieved it and covered her body.

Hearing movement in the hallway Grant grabbed a couple bags of blood and decided to see who was also awake. He gently closed the door behind him hoping not to wake Elise then turned to walk down the steps when Roman was standing behind him with arms folded across his chest.

"It's not what it looks like sir," he blurted out, nervously. He wasn't sure why but he felt embarrassed that Roman knew Elise was sleeping in his room. They were adults and didn't have to hide. But at the same time Grant was wondering what exactly he was trying to hide. Nothing happened between them and they were not dating. Plus that moment in the kitchen would probably never happen again.

"I was just coming to check on you. Lucas and Santiago said you fell ill and they fed you bags of blood to replenish what you lost. They carried you to your room for rest and Elise refused to leave your side," Roman explained.

"I do not understand. There was no blood loss; I was simply practicing my telepathic abilities when I became ill," Grant said confused.

"Ah, but it is energy and mind power that you have never used before which drains the nutrients from your body. Using mind control or telepathy consumes more blood than usual which is why you must be prepared for such activity ahead of time. Elise knows this and she should have had you properly prepare," Roman said sternly.

"It wasn't her fault. I insisted on trying to send her a message and it worked on the first try. I was really excited and wanted to continue. I apologize for my ignorance," Grant said ashamed.

Roman knew exactly what happened between them in the kitchen. He had read it in Grant's mind however respectfully he did not want to interfere with how well their relationship was progressing. Standing in the hallway were two men staring at each other not knowing what to say regarding the sleeping woman behind Grant's door and Roman knowing the things he wanted to do to her.

"Very well. Follow me. It's time to talk business," Roman announced and walked down the hall with his cape flowing behind, not waiting for Grant.

****

In Roman's office the two men sat face to face in chairs closest to the fireplace. Roman had offered him a glass of wine but Grant had refused. His head was still aching from his telepathy session and thought wine would make it worse.

"I visited your business partner, Ethan Hardwicke in the daylight hours. I wanted to be sure he didn't know about your new lifestyle and I offered him the proposal we had agreed on."

Grant was not surprised that he had taken over the assignment that they had miserably failed. It was Grant's job to meet with his partner and offer him the proposal but Elise couldn't resist verbally attacking Mona. He was embarrassed his first mission was a bust.

"How did Ethan take the news?" Grant asked curiously.

"I stuck exactly to our arranged plans. First, I told him that you had passed away and left me as beneficiary to your personal belongings and part ownership of the company. He was not happy about that but after offering him triple the amount of what his half the company was worth he walked away without blinking an eye. I was curious to see what his plans were to do with the money so I read his mind. Apparently, he has had a gambling problem for the last two years and was…how they say it, broke as a joke," Roman said as he studied Grant's reaction intently.

Grant was shocked to hear that his lifelong friend and business partner had been living a double life. How could he not have noticed? Obviously, he did not have the same ambitions for the company as much as Grant did. Another disappointment Grant was faced with since turning into a vampire.

"Mr. Hardwicke is now a retiree on a plane to Tahiti in hiding from all of the people he owes money to. I had my people draw up the paperwork before he left and you and I are official business partners."

Grant agreed to the prearranged plan but felt unclear as to how sharing the company with him would really work out. Yes, he did agree to Roman buying out his partner and to have part ownership of the company but why did Roman want an auto company?

"I was wondering when you would ask that question Mr. Biltmore," Roman said after reading Grant's mind.

Grant rolled his eyes at the annoyance of having his mind read. He would need to train with Elise on how to guard thoughts around other immortals.

"The Cantonelli's have gained many friends and business partners through the years. That is how we built up our mighty empire. Don't worry you will meet all of them when the Council visits in six months. With that said, luxury vehicles would not only be a perk to use personally, but your company would also give current and future vampires a place of employment. I believe in growing our assets to ensure a prosperous future for our immortal children. It is no secret that money drives the universe. There is not much you can do without it, and when you live past the normal life expectancy of a mortal planning a secure financial future for oneself is crucial," Roman tried to explain in a way Grant would understand.

Grant now understood that the price for Roman turning him was to give up his company to existing and future vampires. He built that company from the ground up and the thought of just handing it over to people he just met was a bit troubling. Grant had controlled almost everything in the company and it would be hard to sit back and watch changes being made. However, he was given the gift of living forever and having supernatural powers. Shared ownership was the agreement so Grant would have half power over any implementations and ideas.

He thought back to the day he was taken from his office, and remembered the vehicle they placed him in. The décor, organized layout, and quality of the furnishings were very impressive. It was literally a mobile hospital fit for kings. All of that equipment, lighting, and flooring came from the best brands and he could understand the monetary worth of it. Roman obtaining an auto company was going to save the immortal family millions of dollars in transportation costs globally.

"I'm beginning to put the pieces together of how this operation will work and how it would benefit you. Forgive me for intruding on financial affairs, however I was under the impression that money was no object for immortals."

"You are a very smart man, Grant. Your wheels have been turning in that mind of yours in the correct direction. Another prime example of why the Council wanted you in the immortal family. I can assure you that the Cantonelli family is wealthy beyond your imagination. Most immortals are financially taken care of due to living so long and having multiple careers. Think about it for a moment. Would you want to be a teacher or a factory worker for hundreds of years? Immortals get bored with their jobs just like regular mortals. The opportunity is there to try many professions which allows for successful growth and expertise in many aspects. We really aren't quite that different; we are just more....special," Roman said with a slight grin.

Grant was amazed at how wise, yet reserved Roman acted about how immortals could secretly take over the world if they chose to. He was such a great speaker, he could probably talk anyone into doing what he needed without supernatural powers. The way he explained the logic to people in detail made the vampire life easy to comprehend. The two men were enjoying their conversation together and Grant began to feel that XL Auto would flourish with Roman as a partner. He had many more questions for Roman but he planned to take one step at a time.

"I want you to know that money is not just a hobby the immortals collect like stamps, magnets, or snow globes. We save money because cures for disease and illness for humans do not just magically appear. The world has become a very hard place to live in with new strands of infection popping up each decade. Scientists have to scramble to find vaccines and treatments the first sign of widespread. One important tidbit you need to know is that immortals do not get sick or feel any ailment. Our bodies fight off germs at a rapid rate and also heal almost as the injury has occurred. We have a few human friends that we hold dear. Immortals have had to witness the human race cope with the feelings of sickness and sometimes dying from terminal illness. So the money we acquire and save is research not for us; but for mortals," Roman admitted valiantly.

Roman paused to see if Grant would catch on to what he was getting at. The answer was there however realizing it only came by looking at how all of this fit together downstream. They were talking about many things and Roman suspected Grant was overloaded with information. He started to explain why immortals assist with helping mortals in detail when Grant began talking.

"I'm very impressed with the charity vampires give to mortals," Grant announced as he stood up and walked to the fireplace staring at the glowing embers. He finally understood how immortals viewed the world for all that occupy it.

"Immortals have lived, worked, and mingled with mortals for many years which produced friendships. You have had to watch these people be sick, age, and die while we prosper. You help fund research so the quality of life for mortals can increase and their hardships diminish. The bottom line is vampires are trying to save the human race all across the world," Grant explained while pacing back and forth, talking with his hands.

Grant then looked at Roman for validation of his theory and the smile on his face was proof he was right on target. He couldn't believe that just a few days ago he was one of those research patients fighting for his life. The study he was in was more than likely funded by vampires. The drug he was taking to prolong his existence was created with the help of vampires. He was shocked at how much he had learned about immortals and how essential their role was for the human race. He now felt vampires should be loved and put in the media spotlight instead of hiding in the shadows.

"Now wait a minute before you go thinking we ride in on white stallions carrying all the answers. We are predators that hunt for blood and feed off mortals to survive. Mortals have to be kept alive and healthy because we need them for nourishment. We are viewed as monsters because Rogue vampires choose to kill innocent people and leave horrible images purposely in their mind to fear all vampires. Not all immortals are good and helping cure mortals is not just to give them a good life, but to also keep us alive," Roman spoke honestly.

****

Elise slowly opened her eyes and stretched her legs when she realized she had fallen asleep in Grant's room. She quickly rose from the lounge chair flinging the throw blanket on the floor looking at the empty bed that Grant was sleeping in. Worry quickly consumed her as she thought he didn't make it from their telepathy session and his need for increased blood. She ran for the door stumbling over her feet, just as Bartholomew was opening it. He could sense her uneasiness all the way down the hall in his room and rushed to find her.

"Bart, where is Grant?" she asked with her hand over her once beating heart. She stared into Bart's big brown eyes hoping for good news.

"He is in your uncle's office and they are talking business. Calm down he is ok," Bart said soothingly as he placed a hand on her shoulder.

"That's a relief. I thought something bad happened to him since our telepathy session turned ugly. I should have remembered that he needed extra blood before practicing. I don't know what is wrong with me. First I ruin our first assignment after Grant's turn and then he passes out from sending me messages," Elise said very distraught.

Bartholomew understood completely what was happening to her. As her brother figure he needed to get her grounded. He sat her down on the cushioned bench in the hallway and tried to think how to explain it so she wouldn't get upset.

"Elise, you are like a sister to me and I have been seeing a difference in you ever since Mr. Biltmore became an immortal and moved in. I believe in fate and that everyone has a purpose in this world. I also believe that Grant is your destiny and the connection between you two is immeasurable. I could only wish that I would be lucky enough to find someone to spend eternity with," Bart said as he cupped her hands.

Staring at the floral patterned wallpaper and large sconces lined in the hallway, she was stunned as she realized Bart was absolutely right. She had let her guard down and was distracted from work ever since she met Grant simply because she was falling in love. Immortals spend almost their whole existence searching for the right person to spend eternity with and just like that it had hit her in the face. Grant's personality and the way he stood tall and confident lured her in from the start. His wit and quick understanding of the most complicated issues was most attractive and not to mention he was very pleasing to the eye.

Elise knew that Bart could hear her thoughts so there was no reason for her to say anything. She wrapped her arms around his huge neck, thanking him for his brotherly advice. She knew what she needed to do and stood up jogging down the hall toward the elevator and pushed the level one button. She needed to find out if Grant felt the same way about her. A face to face conversation is what they both needed instead of reading each other's minds or sending telepathic messages.

CHAPTER NINE

Lucas and Santiago were sitting in the elongated conference room, busy working on tracking a confirmed Rogue. They had three stilled images on the plasma screens and were on a conference call with another enforcer, Kieron on their payroll in Toronto. Kieron was a very talented vampire who specialized in technology. If a computer needed hacking or immediate satellite surveillance of a Rogue around the globe he was the man. Not so good with people or mind control, Roman offered him a more indirect position with the Cantonelli family.

Elise was passing the conference room intentionally avoiding eye contact when Lucas noticed her and motioned her inside for assistance.

"Elise we've got word that a Rogue vampire was killed just fifteen minutes from our estate. Now usually I'm thrilled that a worthless piece of trash no longer exists however it seems his killer was a...

mortal. We need everyone on this and Roman needs to be informed," Lucas stated.

This was the worst possible time for work to rear its ugly head. She needed to speak to Grant about her feelings for him however it's not often a Rogue is killed by a mortal. It is usually the other way around.

"OK, I will go alert uncle and meet you in the garage. I'll drive the tech van, you guys get set up in the back with the computers and get Kieron online. We need his eyes and ears," Elise commanded.

Lucas began packing up laptops, files, and phones to head to the garage while Elise got ready. Santiago made his way to the kitchen to prepare a cooler of bagged blood just in case they were out for a long time.

Elise stopped by her room and grabbed her backpack filling it with weapons, her cell phone, and car keys before making her way to the elevator to her uncle's office. The elevator dinged and the doors slid open on level two. Standing at his closed office door she could sense Grant was inside and her stomach felt like butterflies had invaded. Before her uncle realized she was there, she quickly knocked twice then heard her uncle's response to enter.

Grant and Roman stopped their conversation as Elise entered and they both could tell something was wrong. They stood up giving her their full attention and on alert.

"Hello, Grant. I'm glad to see you are well. Uncle, we've received word that a Rogue was killed by mortal hands near the estate. Lucas, Santiago, and I are going to look for the mortal per your approval. We'll have Kieron be our eyes while mobile," Elise said as she looked back and forth between the men.

"I don't like this situation, Elise. Take care of it and have Bartholomew tag along in case you get into trouble. Call me the moment a problem arises," Roman said as he walked over to his desk turning FangTime on.

Elise nodded in approval of his command and glanced at Grant sending him a telepathic message that she needed to speak with him when she returned. He nodded acknowledging that he heard her message as she closed the door behind her. Grant suddenly felt worried that something would happen to Elise. He understood that he was just turned and was not trained as an enforcer but the urge to protect her made him restless. Pacing the floor and running his hands threw his hair, Grant thought about the day he first laid eyes on her. Facing unknown danger that day, he still thought she was most gorgeous woman he'd ever seen. Then the moment he woke up and saw her sleeping in his room the night he lost consciousness made him smile inside. He could certainly get used to waking up beside her every day. His hands began to sweat just reminiscing about her when the thought struck him motionless. He was falling for his abductor. She was his purple princess; his purple haven.

Roman watched Grant pace the floor and go through the emotions and thoughts. Grant hadn't noticed that Roman had stopped what he was doing just to read his mind until he heard him clear his throat. He quickly turned around remembering he was not alone in the room and felt quite embarrassed that his romantic thoughts of the Grand Vampire's niece were heard.

"No need to be embarrassed. You wouldn't believe all the things we immortals hear from the general public in passing. Elise will be fine and she is trained. That is something you will have to get used to if you form a relationship," Roman admitted before hitting the connect button on the FangTime screen. Due to the situation, their conversation was over and Roman needed to alert the Council of the situation. Since everyone had something to do, Grant decided he would finish unpacking in his suite and then possibly take a walk to clear his mind and think about the information he had learned about immortals and process his feelings for Elise.

Grant watched the enforcer entourage leave the garage from his suite window. He kept reminding himself Elise had been on countless missions and would be ok. Lucas, Santiago, and Bartholomew were with her so that made him feel a little more comfortable. He hadn't a clue about fighting Rogues and yet he wished it was him out there instead of her.

He walked away from the window and focused at the task at hand; hanging his suits. Almost an hour later all of his clothes were hung up, and other items folded neatly in the drawers. All he needed to do now was break down the empty boxes and put them in the garage. Something he could do when he returned from his walk. He had never walked the estate before and wanted to take in the beauty of the landscaping and familiarize himself with his new home.

The mansion was huge and yet it was so empty. He looked for someone to tell that he was going for a walk but everyone was gone. Roman was in a meeting with the Council and the others were off doing detective work. He grabbed a house key that lay on a tray near the entrance and opened the front door welcoming the outside breeze. The sun would be rising soon and he needed to be back inside for blood before that happened.

He walked down the long circled driveway toward the main gates where the hired watchmen guarded the entrance. Seeing him walk toward them alerted their senses then realized he was the newbie and stopped him for small talk. Grant told them he was going to take a short walk around the estate and he would be back before sunrise. He knew they would understand because they too were vampires. The color of their eyes told the story. He wondered if he had ever been near a vampire in his mortal life. Surely he would have noticed the purple colored eyes. Or did they wear colored contacts when among mortals?

To the left of the estate was a long road without a sidewalk. The only traffic would be someone who lived on the estate so he walked in the middle instead of the norm of bearing to the right. He stuffed his hands in his jean pockets and lowered his head watching the pavement as his legs took him onward. He had a whole new life and opportunities within a blink of an eye and he needed time to adjust. He died, became a vampire, faked a death, moved, and obtained a new business partner all within one week. To make the situation more complicated he had developed feelings for the Grand Vampire's niece.

The more he thought about Elise he couldn't help but feel that he was destined for this lifestyle. Living for eternity was a great power to have although without the right people in your life, it could be very lonely. He hadn't thought about the possibility of never being able to marry or have children and now the thought of not experiencing either one was disappointing. After all the vampires he had met so far were not married and there certainly were no babies living on the estate. His new family hadn't talked about such things except for Roman's odd comment about securing the future for immortal children. He wondered what that comment really meant.

He enjoyed the short time he has had with Elise and he definitely felt a vibe or energy between them especially the night of their telepathic session when she had just showered and her hair was wet and her skin glowed its natural beauty. He was sure she was a princess in her mortal life. He wondered if she felt attraction for him and if vampires could have an intimate relationship. He really needed to talk to Santiago for answers to these questions. He wouldn't dare feel comfortable asking Elise if vampires can love and make a family.

Grant, deep in thought did not hear the footsteps behind him and before it was too late a heavy object came crashing down on his head. His body fell in the middle of the road and his head crashed on the pavement. All Grant saw was darkness and his ears rang like a school bell from the pain. His head throbbed and became disoriented fast but also wondered as to who and why someone would attack him. If only he could send a message to someone to help him but the pain was too severe for him to focus and he didn't know the gate watchmen's names. He heard the person shouting at him in such an angry tone and the voice sounded so familiar.

His body was trying to heal itself but he was losing a lot of blood fast. He needed help. He didn't know if a telepathic message would travel to Elise being so far away but he had to try in case it was his last words. It would probably use up the last of his energy but he had to try to reach her. Grant cleared his mind trying to block the pain and said Elise's name and the word "I need you," before he lost consciousness.

Luckily the watchmen at the gate were also vampires and smelled fresh blood in the downward wind. They were not supposed to leave their post however they knew Grant could be in trouble and could not yet defend himself. Within seconds after Grant blacked out, the two men wrestled the attacker to the ground and secured his hands behind his back with zip ties. They would have used mind control or the sleep charm but the attacker was the same gender as them, male. One of the watchmen pulled out a cell phone and called over the intercom system inside the estate to alert code black procedures.

The other watchmen picked up the attacker as if he was a feather and started to carry him to the main gates for Roman to assess and give the orders on what to do with him.

The watchmen pocketed his phone and then turned his attention to Grant who was hurt very badly. He needed to get him to the mansion promptly for blood or he was not going to survive. He scooped him up in his arms and ran at lightning speed to get him medical attention. The watchmen were trained for situations such as this and would do whatever they could to help a fellow vampire; especially from a mortal attack.

****

Elise, Lucas, and Santiago whisked to the scene of the reported Rogue attack while Kieron backtracked satellite images at the precise moment the Rogue was killed. They already had a lot of evidence which proved the attacker was inexperienced and sloppy. Kieron saved the images on his computer and wiped the satellites memory of the seven minute ordeal. The general public could not find out the victim was a vampire.

Santiago read the minds of two mortal witnesses who called it in to emergency services. The policewoman that took their statements was mortal so their task of concealing the truth became harder. Santiago put a sleep charm on the police officer to get the report. The witnesses statement explained that an older man was following the younger man walking down the street as if he was stalking him and then pulled a sickle out of his inside coat pocket and beheaded him. The attacker then quickly fled into a nearby alley and the witnesses called 911.

Lucas volunteered to wipe the memories from the witnesses as they had to be sure that this incident was contained. They were made to believe they saw children playing with imaginary swords and sent them on their way. Santiago snatched the report and tucked it away to give to Roman back at the estate. Elise tended to the vampire while the other enforcers were busy trying to look for some form of ID. She had to work quickly because the body was turning to dust as the sun peaked over the horizon. Roman had explained to her that a vampire's body turns to dust simply to become debris in the wind. She found a wallet with the victim's name and address.

"Well, Mr. Harrison of West 18th street, looks like your eternal Rogue life was no match for the elderly," Elise said shaking her head in disbelief.

She thought it was odd for the attacker to behead a vampire as if knowing that was the only way to kill a vampire. It was alarming that the attacker knew the younger man was a vampire, which only made matters worse. This killing was very brutal and desperate. If only she knew the attacker's motivation.

"Elise, I have a visual of the attacker. He is near the estate and... just attacked his second victim. Estate ground control has just issued a code black," Kieron said in the earpiece she was wearing.

She quickly yelled for Lucas and Santiago to get back in the van and hunt this guy down when she received a telepathic message from Grant. She could barely hear it but his tone sounded urgent. Realizing he was pleading for help she had to get to him fast.

"Oh no, guys! It's Grant! He's been hurt and we need to get back to the estate fast!" she told the enforcers from the back of the van with tears in her eyes.

****

Inside the estate was utter chaos. Roman ordered the watchmen to put the attacker in the steel cell until he tended to Grant's wounds. He felt terrible for leaving Grant alone and not realizing he had left the mansion. New vampires were naïve to potential threats and the guilt he felt was unbearable. He would never forgive himself as Grant was not only the future Grand Vampire but also Elise's future husband. Roman worked feverishly to get Grant situated in the hospital room with IV bags of blood and syringes filled with pain medicine. The wound on his head was deep enough for him to possibly have a cracked skull which would take longer for the body to heal.

He needed his enforcers to help stabilize Grant but was afraid to inform Elise about what happened. He knew how they felt about each other and he didn't want Elise to resent him for allowing the attack to occur.

Roman's cell phone began to ring.

"Yes?" Roman answered.

"How bad is Grant? Is he conscious? Where is the attacker?" Elise asked panicked.

"It's pretty serious and no he is out cold. The attacker is in the cell guarded by the gate watchmen. I need you all here, now!" Roman ordered.

"We are two minutes away and will help with whatever you need. I'm so scared, Uncle."

"I know you are, sweetheart. Everything is going to be fine. One question, how did you know Grant was attacked?"

"Grant sent me a telepathic message asking for help. Why?"

"Your bond is even more powerful than I thought. That's excellent news."

"You are hiding something from me. What is it?"

Just then Grant started to wake up from the immense pain, vomited and began to moan loudly. Elise could hear him through the phone. Not having time to talk, Roman ended the call abruptly to administer more pain meds to him. It was going to be a rough day in the Cantonelli home.

CHAPTER TEN

It was already nine in the morning and Grant went through five bags of blood and three doses of pain medicine. The watchmen had returned to their post once the enforcers arrived. Of course Elise ran straight to the hospital room to see the extent of Grant's injuries with Bart running behind her for support. Her first look at Grant sleeping with obvious pain on his face and the hole on the top of his head smacked her with reality and she crumbled into Bart's arms sobbing.

"How could I have let this happen?" she shrieked.

Bart held her tight and stroked her hair as she cried on his gigantic shoulder. He let her cry and cry some more until her tears finally dried. Lucas and Santiago crept into the room to check on Grant and saw how upset Elise was. They never saw her so upset over an attack of a newbie and wondered if Elise and Grant had a romantic connection and would be a couple, if he lived.

Roman bolted into the room ordering all the enforcers except for Elise to follow him to the steel cell to interrogate the attacker. They followed their leader dutifully to the secured cell and watched Roman punch in the code for the doors to open. Their first impression was that the attacker was nothing but a feeble old man and was surely senile. However the images that flashed into Roman's mind told a different story involving Grant and other vampires he had known. Roman's eyes began to glow as he sifted through the attackers mind from the day he was born, graduated medical school, and finally the reason for the attack; seeing a vampire for the first time.

"His name is Dr. Leo Rowland and he knew Grant from the experimental therapy study he was participating in. It was the blood work that alerted him to Grant' s new lifestyle and of course being a doctor he researched textbooks and mythological books until wee hours of the morning looking for a logical explanation. It seems he has been tracking suspected vampires in hopes to be bitten and live forever. If they vampires refused to turn him, he would kill them." Roman said to the group in disgust.

Everyone stood in silence staring at this wrinkled, gray haired old man shocked of his actions. They occasionally came across desperate people every couple of years who discovered their secret and wanted to be like them so badly they risked their careers, family, and sometimes their life.

"Let's destroy this scumbag," Bartholomew said as he inched toward Dr. Rowland.

"We should wait until Grant wakes up and let him have a say in the punishment. He knew the guy and may want to help save his life or help end it," Lucas suggested as he stopped Bart with his arm.

"Very well. Keep him in the cell until Grant wakens. Bartholomew, get our prisoner some food to keep him nourished. Even though I ache to see him suffer for what he did, the Council respects the Cantonelli's for our moral standards." Roman ordered.

****

Elise rubbed Grant's arm back and forth as she watched him rest. The pain medicine was finally working and he seemed very peaceful. Occasionally he would move his head to find a more comfortable position. She looked at the wound on his head and it appeared to be shrinking and the blood was drying up. She was no doctor but all signs were looking good that he would survive.

Her reaction to him being injured startled her as she couldn't imagine falling in love with someone she had just met less than two weeks ago. But he made her feel so happy inside. Every day she would wake up in anticipation of seeing and teaching him the ways of vampire life. The more she got to know him, the more she wanted him for herself. Ironically they shared the same timeline of events. She was turned against her will and so was he.

The night of their first telepathy session she felt like she had known him all of her life. The chemistry between them was so hot she had wanted to pounce on him and drag him to her room for a night of body exploring. Realizing she was getting herself worked up enough that her eyes were glowing she stood up and walked to the window that faced the main entrance. Gazing out across the lawn surrounded by iron fencing around the whole estate, reminded her that threats on their lives would never stop and they would be on guard for eternity. That was such a sad feeling however if you were lucky enough to find that special someone that made everything worth fighting for, the reality of immortality problems seemed so worth it.

"Elise…" Grant moaned as he shook his head slowly back and forth trying to fight off the grogginess.

She quickly rushed to his side and offered soothing sounds from her mouth.

"Sssh, you rest now. I'm here with you and not going anywhere ever again," She reassured him.

"Someone attacked me. I tried to send you a message," Grant slurred slowly with his eyes remained closed.

Elise tried to remain strong however a single tear fell down her cheek as she answered, "I heard your message and I came as quickly as I could."

Grant mustered enough energy for a smile and then fell into a deep slumber. His body was healing nicely but the severe injury to his head would take more time and blood. Santiago had called ahead to the warehouse for them to send an extra blood supply shipment in preparation for his recovery.

Elise grabbed a bag of blood and placed it on her fangs. She needed to keep herself fresh and healthy in order to get Grant fully well. The bag was empty in seconds and she felt very satisfied. She was very bored but didn't want to leave the room so she turned the TV on and ironically a teen vampire show was on. She laughed out loud at their ridiculous appearance and awful impersonations. *If only they knew what a real vampire was like, she thought.*

Several hours had passed and it was almost three o'clock in the afternoon. She must have dozed off while watching TV and noticed it was turned off. Bart must have come in to check on them during nap time- she noticed that the refrigerator was freshly stocked with blood and extra blankets and pillows folded neatly on the couch. He was a very thoughtful vampire.

****

In the conference room sat Roman, Lucas, Santiago, and Bartholomew staring at the screen which showed all the Council members in attendance. Kieron was on speakerphone giving a blow by blow description on how he located the attacker and dispatched the enforcers. The Council was very pleased with his prompt attention and commended his work. Lucas and Santiago gave a summary of their actions and read the full police report out loud. As they suspected, the report would be destroyed so no record or memories of the incident would ever surface again. There was one issue that was left unresolved, which was deciding the fate of Dr. Leo Rowland.

Roman explained to the Council the images he saw in Dr. Rowland's mind and they were very surprised with the doctor's persistence at finding the answers to the mysteries. At the same time they were very discouraged of his planned violence on their immortal family. After several moments of the members whispering back and forth they came to a decision of the action needed for their prisoner. The enforcers and Grand Vampire listened to their decision and had no choice but to accept and nod in agreement.

One of the members asked how serious Grant's injuries were and if Roman needed their assistance with anything. Roman explained that Grant would heal and that he had everything under control. He also reassured them that everything was on schedule and looked forward to their visit in the next few months.

Everyone waved bye to each other and the screen went blank ending their conference.

"Are they insane?" Lucas asked, visibly upset as he stood up and smacked the table with his palm.

"Lucas, they have their reasons and we must respect it. They are very experienced immortals with powers and intuition much stronger than ours. As soon as Grant wakes, we will take care of Dr. Rowland," Roman said sternly.

****

Elise decided that she would go out for a quick hunt. She knew the enforcers were having a meeting with the Council and should not be disturbed. Before exiting the front door she wrote a note for her uncle that said "Be back soon, I'm hungry". The cool evening air blew the leaves across the driveway and she remembered her mortal childhood days of collecting leaves for crafts. Her Mother would let her make collages of her favorite colored leaves and then hang them on the fridge until winter. The red ones were her favorite which just happened to be the color of her future meals.

As a little girl she dreamed of having the perfect wedding and having a couple of children. She wondered if she would ever get to have a family someday. When she was first turned and realized her lifestyle had changed she was afraid of never having a normal life but her Uncle assured her that vampires could love, marry, and have children just like mortals. The only difference was that a vampire being in love was more powerful because it created a lifetime bond with their chosen life mate until their soul no longer existed. Vampires never divorced or separated because destiny didn't allow the opportunity. When they found that special someone it was as if fate gave the "greenlight" to reproduce and carry on the family name. Fertility did not begin until a vampire was truly in love. The immortal childbearing rule was that a female vampire should only be pregnant with child every fifteen years to ensure proper care of the child, training on immortality, schooling, and overall family bonding time before starting their own life. Babies would have to learn how to live in a mortal world and keep their powers a secret. The world was not ready for mortals and vampires to live in unity.

Elise made her way to her favorite hunting spot, found a donor and quenched her thirst. She always made sure to wipe their memory and replace it with a positive one. Her goal was to feed and then release the mortal without reading their mind. Getting attached to prey was not professional and it allowed opportunities of getting caught off guard and being attacked once the mortal awakened from mind control.

As the crescent moon made its way into its position in the night sky she returned to the estate and found a pleasant surprise inside Grant's room. He had a concussion but was alert and talking. All the enforcers were gathered around his hospital bed telling jokes to help keep his spirits up until Elise returned. She sent each enforcer a telepathic message thanking them for caring after Grant while she was away then stepped farther into the room to get a look at Grant's wound.

"How was your hunt?" Grant asked with a slight grin.

Elise smiled back and said it was scrumptious. She would have to take him soon on his first hunt instead of drinking from bags. She explained how warm blood tasted much better than chilled blood that has been kept in a refrigerator.

"Grant, it is wonderful to see you in such high spirits after being attacked but we must get down to business. We captured your attacker and he is currently being held in our cell," Santiago said in a serious tone.

Grant was relieved that the immortal was caught and no longer feared for his or another immortals safety. Reading his mind, Santiago shook his head no at his accusation.

"No, what?" Grant asked.

"Your attacker was mortal and it just so happens that when Roman read his mind you were in some of his images. Grant, I do not want to upset you but this attacker is Dr. Rowland," Santiago said as he studied Grant's face for reaction.

Stunned in disbelief he closed his eyes then bowed his head for a moment to gather his thoughts. How could he have been so stupid as to not remember that Dr. Rowland was the first person who had clues that Grant was different? Most importantly why would the doctor who worked tirelessly to keep him alive, try to kill him in the end?

"Grant it isn't your fault. We should have found him and erased any memories of you in his mind. All of the enforcers take full responsibility for leaving loose ends," Bart said, reading his thoughts.

"Dr. Rowland researched your lab results, studied textbooks, and dabbled in mythology which led him to the truth. You were not his only immortal patient and he was beginning to realize the trend. It turned into an obsession for him to become immortal himself so he began stalking his patients with abnormal results in hopes they would bite him to be turned," Lucas explained.

His mouth hung open as he tried to imagine the desperation of a mortal seeking to find a vampire for the chance at living forever. Since he had been involuntarily turned he could not feel that level of want.

Elise could tell the news was hitting him hard and sent him a message saying that he had a new family now that would protect and love him for all eternity. She hoped he was getting her hint that it was she that loved him.

Bart sensed the need for Elise and Grant to have a moment of privacy and took the lead in getting Lucas and Santiago to help him with the attacker. Realizing what Bart was up to they followed his lead and wished Grant well as they left the room.

"I thought they would never leave," Grant said smiling.

"I know what you mean. You had me pretty scared back there. I was so upset that I would never have the chance to tell you...." Elise said as her voice began to crack from holding in emotion.

"I love you too, Elise." Grant said as he cupped her face with the palm of his hand.

Elise had tears running down her cheeks as Grant raised his hand to wipe them away and kissed the top of her hand.

"The moment I met you I felt a connection and I fought it because you had just became a vampire. Then that night in the kitchen I wanted you so badly," She said.

"Then I passed out, and I got attacked..." Grant said as he rolled his eyes in humor.

Elise smiled as he was making light of the situation. She loved that he could read her fear but say the right words to give her instant comfort. She leaned in close to Grant that her lips grazed his and the moisture made their skin stick together. Unable to resist, Grant raised his upper body and took her lips fully into his. The passion between them caused both of their eyes to glow. They closed their eyes to savor the moment and Elise lost control and couldn't get enough of him. She climbed up on the hospital bed straddling him then placed her hands around the sides of his face only to kiss him deeper.

"I have never felt this way about anyone before and I want to please you now," he said in a whisper in between kisses.

Grant moaned as he was still in pain and Elise was his medicine. Grabbing the back of her head he caressed her neck all the way to her collarbone. Her body arched back inviting him to explore further. She leaned her head back and released a sound of pleasure as one of his hands gripped her breasts while the other hand unhooked her bra. He teased her buds with his thumbs as she bit her lip from crying out. His hardness he felt for her was throbbing and he desperately needed more of her. He rose from the hospital bed, unhooked his IV and laid her gently down on his bed as he undressed her.

She began to feel nervous as she realized they were actually going to make love. He was the first intimate experience she had ever had. Reading her mind Grant stopped and tilted his head surprised that she had never been intimate. Sensing him hesitate, she sent him a message begging him not to stop and that she wanted to be with him forever.

With a wave of her hand Elise turned the lights down low and started the fireplace by the turn of the knob on the wall. Supernatural powers were great to have for spur of the moment occasions such as this. Amused as she flaunted her talents he consumed her body as they rocked back and forth. They kissed intently as a rush of excitement exploded and both of their fangs retracted. As if knowing what should happen next, they both leaned down to each other's necks and pierced skin as their fangs drank from each other's blood.

Sensing she had taken enough Elise released the hold of him as a sign he needed to do the same. Her warm blood tasted so good in his mouth which made him feel like a hunter. She felt so good sexually and his lips tingling after biting her made him not want to stop but he also feared of taking too much of her blood. He filled her with his fluid as she moaned in her own pleasure while scratching his back to gain control. They had just made love and bonded as vampire life mates.

According to the immortal lifestyle they were now considered a couple which should be formally announced with a wedding.

Now all Elise had to do was break the news to him as he didn't realize what they just did usually lead to holy matrimony.

CHAPTER ELEVEN

"Bartholomew, gather Lucas and Santiago and tell them to meet me in the backup hospital room." Roman said as he walked quickly around the mansion getting the needed supplies.

Roman had to fulfill the Council's decision of turning Dr. Rowland into a vampire. He did not like the idea of having to turn the attacker of the future Grand Vampire but he had no choice. The Council decided it would be beneficial to have more doctors in the immortal family and since his mind would have to be wiped clean anyway this would be Dr. Rowland's chance at another life.

In the last decade or so they've had to wipe three mortal minds clean after they discovered vampires were real and walking among them. Roman would brief the Council on the situation and they would decide their fate. If they thought the mortal would be of use to the immortal family they would order the mortal to be turned into a vampire in which Roman would train and teach them the new lifestyle.

Roman did not like the fact that the doctor attacked vampires hoping they would turn him and now he would be getting what he wanted. This was not a punishment for him, it was a reward. Roman was in the foulest moods and felt nothing could happen that would make this day better.

****

Elise woke up to her head on Grant's chest and then wedged her head in-between his neck and chin. With her eyes closed and smiling she remembered their intimate encounter and was sure that he was the perfect person to spend eternity with.

Grant slowly stirred and opened his eyes staring at the beautiful blonde that lay next to him. Their love making made him feel weaker but he fell more in love with her at the same time.

"Are you awake?" he asked as he roped her in tighter with his arm.

"Yes. How do you feel?" she asked.

"I feel pretty weak and hungry."

"I'm so sorry it's my entire fault. I shouldn't have overexerted you while you are recovering." She explained as she got up and was picking her clothes of the ground.

Grant smiled as he watched his beautiful woman quickly put clothes on as if she was embarrassed for him to see her.

"Elise, I think we are past the awkward phase. There is no need to be nervous with me. You're beautiful in every way." He said

Elise smiled as she bent down to kiss him then opened the refrigerator and grabbed two bags, one for herself. The smell of blood caused his fangs to instantly descend.

"So what does this mean for us now? Are we boyfriend and girlfriend?"

Avoiding the question she quickly popped the bag of blood onto his fangs then explained she had to go to work and would check in on him later as she walked out the door and quickly closed it behind her.

Grant was surprised at her peculiar behavior. *Maybe she was afraid of commitment he thought?*

****

Elise was in the kitchen making her some coffee when Bart walked in as if he was on a mission.

"What's going on, Bart?" she asked.

"Oh I haven't seen you to let you know we are turning the prisoner now. You'd better get down there in the event we need a sleep charm or mind control. You are the only female in the house."

Bart gathered what he came in for and then rushed out of the room to the elevator.

Elise's coffee would have to wait. She was not going to miss the turn of her man's attacker. She hoped it would be painful and agonizing turn for what he did to Grant. Rushing out of the room she caught up to Bart at the elevator as the doors just began to open. They boarded and pushed the Level 3 button and waited patiently for the doors to close.

"Congratulations, by the way." Bart said staring at the lighted dots move on the elevator.

"Is it that obvious that we mated?" Elise asked shyly.

"You are positively glowing inside. Everyone will be able to see how happy you are." Bart said as he hugged her.

She hugged him back and thanked him for always being there for her and hoped that someday he would be able to experience the pure joy of finding that special someone.

The elevator pinged and the doors opened to their destination and they quickly changed their mood into a professional enforcer on a mission. Turning someone was a very delicate process and they had to be prepared for any emergency. Sometimes although very rare the person being turned would not be able to be controlled and would attack the immortals trying to turn them. In those cases it turned out the mortal had a preexisting mental condition and the transition enhanced their symptoms causing absolute mania.

Then there were cases that a mortal turned but never woke up again. The Council described it as nature's way of declining their position into immortality and that their soul needed peace. It was sad situations when that occurred because some immortals admired and loved the people they intended to turn.

Opening the cell door that Dr. Rowland was waiting in Elise took one look at him and the anger of him attacking Grant almost consumed her. She saw an old, wrinkly heavy set man with long white shoulder length hair.

"You ugly piece of sh…." She said as she drew her arm back to punch him in the face.

Roman was standing behind her when this happened and used mind control to stop her cold in her tracks. He sent her a message to calm her saying that the circumstances were unfortunate however this was destiny's plan from the beginning. We may not understand why he has been elected to join immortality but the Council never makes bad decisions.

Lucas and Santiago approached Roman and said the room was ready for Dr. Rowland to be moved into. Roman nodded acknowledging that he heard them and released the hold on Elise. It was then that he realized why Elise was so emotional about Grant. He could see the radiance of pure joy and the new intimate bond between Grant and her. Roman smiled at his niece and sent her a congratulatory message of finding her life mate.

Elise smiled as she felt embarrassed that her uncle could tell she lost her innocence just hours ago. Then again secrets were constantly unveiled because of the mind reading powers. Sometimes being able to read minds were a curse as thoughts being heard weren't always pleasant.

Getting back to the task at hand Roman turned around abruptly causing his cape to swirl behind him. It was time to initiate the turn and celebration would have to come later.

"Bring him to the room." Roman ordered to Elise.

Elise's eyes began to glow as she gained control of Dr. Rowland's mind as she ordered his body to stand up and walk in front of her. Dr. Rowland could see and hear what was going on but was numb from being able to react to it. She sent him into the room and told him to lay on the hospital bed as she locked the door behind them.

Inside Lucas, Santiago, and Bart were waiting around the hospital bed and once the doctor was in position they strapped him down for their safety. Elise released control over the doctor so he could be fully aware of what was happening however she silenced him by placing an imaginary lock on his lips so he could not speak.

Dr. Rowland was petrified that the vampires would torture him and perform painful experiments on him. After all the books he rented from the library fictional tales stated what happens to mortals who discover their secret. Everyone stood around the hospital bed waiting for Roman's orders. Their stern and disapproving faces were evident of the despise they felt for him.

"Dr. Rowland you really need to start renting books that are worth reading and that do not misconstrue the truth. It seems you have gotten your wish to join the immortality family but understand I do not approve nor like you. Your attack on Mr. Biltmore and the other vampire lives you have taken has affected the Cantonelli family that will never be forgiven; however, the Council believes your professional career could be of use to us. When you awaken you will have a choice to accept your new lifestyle or we will turn you to dust." Roman said with his teeth clenched.

Roman gave the signal to Santiago and half a second later Santiago's fangs had hold of Dr. Rowland's throat. The pain was excruciating as Santiago made sure he was not gentle. Since Elise had silenced his mouth, the screams could not be heard but he still opened his mouth to try and yell. This moment was payback for the harm he caused to immortals and they relished in his pain.

After several moments, Santiago retreated once he was sure he had bitten and taken enough of his blood and Lucas handed him a towel to wipe his mouth. They all waited for obvious signs of body distress but Dr. Rowland had gone unconscious from the excitement alone. Roman ordered Bartholomew to stay and monitor him for any signs of complication of the turn and he was to notify Roman at once for any problems.

CHAPTER TWELVE

Grant awoke from another nap since Elise had left him in his room. He wasn't planning on falling asleep but his body must have needed more time to heal. His head no longer throbbed and he was feeling much better. Reaching his hand to his injury he noticed the hole was now closed but was still a little tender and bumpy. He decided a nice long shower was what he needed to feel refreshed.

Grant returned to his suite to enjoy his oversized shower room. He grabbed a towel from the linen closet and undressed leaving his clothes on the bedroom floor. He still had dried up blood on his head and face from the attack and it was matted in his hair. Before stepping into the shower he turned on some music from the sound system encased in the wall. He turned it up and stepped under the shower head letting the water cascade down his back. As he washed his body starting with his genitals, he immediately thought of Elise.

He couldn't wait to see her again and wondered how Roman would take their new relationship.

An upbeat tempo song came on that he used to listen to all the time. He didn't know the band's name but knew the lead singer was a woman. Her voice was amazing and imagined there was no song she couldn't sing. He began to sing along with the words as he dipped his head back to wet his hair when the shower curtain moved back and Elise stepped in with him naked.

Surprised and glad to see her he wrapped his arms around her and began to kiss her neck and swayed to the music.

"You like this song, huh?" she asked.

"I love this song and would listen to it all the time in my office and car in my mortal days." Grant said.

Elise smiled and kissed him passionately as the water flowed between their bodies.

"I can get you a signed copy of that song from Vanessa Rose if you want. We are pretty close." She said smirking.

"Are you kidding me? I would love that."

"Ok, I'll sign a cd for you later." She said as she laid her head on his chest letting the words sink in.

Grants eyebrows rose as he realized she had just told him she made the song. He grabbed both of her arms and held her back at arm's length staring at her in disbelief. She started giggling at his stunned reaction.

"You are Vanessa Rose? They play it on the radio all the time, you know?"

"Yes, I know. I am signed under Crimson Records. I have a contract that any new music gets played on the radio twice every three hours. To top it off, I accomplished it all without having to use mind control."

Grant was amazed at his new rock star girlfriend that words could not express how he felt; so he showed her. He kissed her all over her body occasionally sucking in the water that rested on her skin. She closed her eyes as he pleased her until she exploded in ecstasy. Trying to catch her breath she needed to tell Grant the truth about their relationship before it went any further. He needed to know they were technically married according to the immortal lifestyle and wasn't sure how he would take it.

"Grant, I need to tell you something." Elise said as the water continued to run.

"What? Are you an astronaut too?" he said jokingly.

"No, when we made love it created a special bond between us. Whenever immortals take a step further of intimacy it is destiny bringing them together for all eternity. I should have explained this to you that night but we got a little out of control." She said red faced.

"I understand what you mean. I haven't been able to get you off my mind since that happened either."

"No, you don't understand. In the immortal lifestyle when a couple bonds mind and body the status of their relationship reaches maximum level. Immortals only have the urge to make love if they have met their soulmate. In the eyes of the Council and immortals everywhere in the world once the relationship has been consummated they are mated for life.....as in marriage."

Grant was totally caught off guard at her announcement and was trying to comprehend what she just said.

"Are you telling me we informally married?" Grant asked in shock.

Elise nodded her head yes and studied his face for a reaction. At one point she almost burst into tears when he just stood there not saying a word and expected his next words to be hurtful.

Grant read her mind and understood the fear she was feeling and grabbed underneath her chin and turned her face up to look at him. He smiled and said, "I have never felt this way about anyone before and although I may no longer be breathing technically speaking, meeting you has breathed life into my soul."

****

The next day all of the enforcers met in the conference room as Roman briefed the Council on the turn of Dr. Rowland. He explained that he made it through the turn and has accepted the immortal lifestyle and training will begin immediately. All of the doctor's family, friends, and coworkers have had all memories of him wiped clean as if he did not exist. The patients he had seen for many years had been visited by the enforcers and given a new doctor's name in their minds as they slept. Lucas personally saw to the moving of the doctor's belongings into the estate where he shall live.

"Dr. Rowland understands that the sole reason he was turned was to provide medical attention to any immortal and in situations when mortals need care." Roman said in closing.

The Council was very pleased with the quick turnaround time of Dr. Rowland's status. They announced that they would be expecting to meet him when they arrive for their visit.

Turning the topic in a different direction the Council asked how Grant was recovering from the attack and transition into immortality. Roman directed the questions to Elise who was sitting right next to him.

"I have information to that question if I may reply sirs." Elise said as she stood up.

Lucas, Santiago, and Bart watched as they heard Elise say, "Grant and I will be formally married during the time of your visit and we respectfully hoped the Council would perform the ceremony."

Cheers were heard all throughout the room on video conference from Italy as the Council rejoiced in her announcement. They accepted the invite and agreed to perform the ceremony which would occur at the estate. The Council was very impressed with how quickly Roman met all of his timelines and was optimistic of the relationship between Elise and Grant. They knew the future of immortals rested in their hands but it was too soon to let them know of the impending trouble.

****

Weeks later, Grant was fully recovered and arranging his belongings into the office that Roman had arranged for him. It was very lavish with the newest technology and of course as a gift, Roman had Lucas create a toy-sized replica of the first vehicle he had acquired right out of college. Grant wondered how Roman would have known that a measly Honda Accord was the first ride he ever had. Then remembered how vampires can filter through memories. He assumed this was a gift from Roman announcing his excitement of their business partnership. He placed the miniature car on the corner of his desk and began to empty the remaining items in a box that he expected the enforcers packed for him the day of his faked death.

Grant was busy positioning all the books, file cabinets, and client files when he sensed someone approach him and turned around quickly thinking it was Elise.

Shocked in disbelief Dr. Rowland stood before him as a vampire with purple eyes. He looked much younger and thinner. The vampire lifestyle suited him well. Assuming he was there to finish his attack Grant's eyes began to glow in anger until Dr. Rowland offered a handshake.

Elise had just gotten out of the meeting when she sensed something was off with Grant and she yelled out for all of the enforcers to follow her to Grant's office. Within seconds they arrived expecting something awful had happened like an intruder when they peered in and found Dr. Rowland and Grant in the same room together. Miraculously they were not fighting but enjoying a glass of wine together.

Elise's perplexed look on her face drew alarm to Grant as he motioned for her to come in. She told the other enforcers it was ok for them to resume to what they were doing and thanked them for following her. She walked into the office and sat down next to Grant as she eyed Dr. Rowland in a hateful manner.

"I wanted you to see for yourself that the doctor and I have mended our relationship and he apologized for attacking me. I understand if you cannot forgive him now, hopefully you might be able to with time."

"How can you sit here and not be upset toward someone for almost ending your immortality?" she asked bewildered.

Dr. Rowland sat in the chair fiddling his thumbs as he looked toward the floor ashamed of what he had done. She was absolutely right that Grant had every right to hate him for the rest of his life. However he was sitting in the office to try and fix the wrong he had done.

Grant looked at Elise and covered her hand with his as he said, "Sweetheart, eternity is a long time and I do not wish to spend it feeling hatred toward every person that has done me wrong. I survived and if you think about it, the injury brought you and me closer. I can't hate him for that."

Elise smiled as she thought she just heard the most beautiful words spoken and was surprised when a warm tear rolled down her cheek. There were many reasons to love this man and his willingness to forgive others made him special. Understanding the two men were safe to be alone together she kissed Grant on the cheek and left the room saying she had a wedding to plan.

CHAPTER THIRTEEN

It had been almost a month since Dr. Rowland's turn and he was fitting in nicely. He had saved an immortal that was attacked by a Rogue in the area. The immortal stayed at the estate for more than a week to recover. With Kieron's help the enforcers tracked him down and relinquished the Rogue.

The Cantonelli home had quieted down once again after getting all of the newbies situated in their new lifestyle. Grant was running his automobile business from home as a silent partner so he would not be noticed by his existing employees. They thought he was just a new owner from out of state. He had messengers and runners that made appearances for him when he needed to handle things directly. Elise had to read the mind of every employee on Grant's payroll to ensure they did not realize their secret. In doing so she uncovered a scheme of at least six employees renting Grant's vehicles out on the weekends and pocketing the money. It had been going on for months without anyone noticing. Grant and Roman fired them on the spot which left them in need of replacements. Roman called a businessman that was also immortal and told him to send six of the best business vampires he knew looking for a job to XL Auto Company and they would be hired on the spot after passing a mind reading test. Everything was coming together according to their business plan and they worked well as a team. Roman was more of a no nonsense boss, where Grant related to his employees more as a mortal since he was just recently turned.

Lucas and Santiago had made two trips to the warehouse to check on blood supply and was pleased to report good findings to Roman. Roman gave them two weeks off for their hard work the past couple months and brought in temporary replacements. Right away they booked airline tickets to go hang out with Kieron in Toronto and spy on people. They envied Kieron for his surveillance toys and skills. They were almost three hundred years old yet they acted like children sometimes.

The Council would be arriving soon and the marriage ceremony would also be taking place. Elise needed help planning the wedding so she called in her enforcer friend Veronica. She needed another woman's advice since Grant was busy with work. He helped when he could but honestly wasn't very good at planning girly things. Veronica was also a beautiful Hispanic immortal that resided in Michigan. She was single and lived in a small condo with her cat. She led a simple vampire life and was thrilled when Elise called for her assistance.

The invitations had just been mailed out, Elise's wedding dress had been flown in from Italy and made by a famous immortal named Vera Wind, flowers had been ordered, and the caterers had been reserved. Almost everything was complete for the wedding and now the focus was on the Council's visit. The Council's visit only happened every one hundred years and the location was different every time. The Cantonelli's were selected to host the World Immortal Conference via live TV and internet on a channel and site mortals could not view. The most eldest of vampires would be in attendance and recognized for their charity efforts.

The estate flourished with gardeners, maids, security, and event planners that additional gate watchmen were hired and getting paid overtime. Everything had to be perfect for the wedding and Council meeting.

Dr. Rowland had organized a surgery, exam room, and lab to be constructed next to the hospital rooms with Roman's approval. He hardly was seen unless he stopped working to feed or meetings with Roman or the enforcers. Every now and then when enforcers had down time they would visit the doctor and look at weird organisms through the microscopes. As a matter of fact the doctor was sure that he had developed a cure for the common flu. Once a person was injected with the magic serum their symptoms were gone in less than an hour and negative results of nasal swabs proved it worked.

****

Grant was in his office when Elise knocked on his door and walked in. He had just finished writing a contract for an immortal businessman and closed his laptop with a wave of his hand.

"Hey there, gorgeous." Grant said as he smiled.

"I was just coming to check on you. You haven't sent me any messages in the last couple hours." She said as she bent over for a hug.

"I'm all finished for today. Anything you would like to do? See a movie, go shopping?" Grant asked.

They both had been busy with work and wedding details but made sure they had quality time together. Their love was so new and strong they could barely get through the work day without the need for each other's touch.

"How about we watch a movie in the theater downstairs? I don't feel up to anything spectacular today."

Grant realized he had never heard her speak so down before.

"Are you alright, my love?"

"I just feel weird. I can't explain it. Immortals do not get sick but I feel as if my body as aching." Elise said nervously.

Grant whisked her right away to be examined by Dr. Rowland. Immortals can experience aches and pains when there was a chance that the bagged blood could have been tainted with an infection or drugs. The blood supply warehouse always screens blood for such issues, however, occasionally it has been known for a bag to get slipped through without being checked.

Grant and Elise found Dr. Rowland relaxing at his lab bench listening to music as his centrifuge machine swirled around with lab samples in it. He saw them come in and turned his chair around to greet them.

"What did I do to deserve this visit?" he asked teasingly.

"Doc, it is Elise. She is ill. Can you check her out?" Grant said in a desperate tone.

"Certainly, lie down and relax." Dr. Rowland said as he got Elise comfortable.

Grant sat in the seat next to Elise's exam table holding her hand while the doctor performed his routine assessment. He looked in her eyes, ears, throat and fangs for any possible signs of receiving a bad bag of blood. So far, everything looked good until he got to her midsection. He poked and prodded around her sides, ribs, and near her navel. He found the source of her problem and straightened in his chair as he glanced at Grant and Elise back and forth not knowing what to say.

Elise could have easily read his mind but respected the need for immortal privacy, however, she was growing rather frustrated at his silence.

"Well, what is it?" she asked rudely.

"Congratulations, you are going to have a baby!" Dr. Rowland announced.

CHAPTER FOURTEEN

After the doctor confirmed her pregnancy and told her she was seven weeks pregnant, she couldn't believe that she was going to be a mother. They weren't formally married yet and she was already pregnant. It was October and the baby would arrive in April. They were both elated at the news but overwhelmed how fast life was moving. Grant asked the obvious questions like does a vampire carry for the full nine months, do they feel labor pains, and will the baby try to feed off the mother. His imagination ran wild with questions and theories. Elise calmed his fears by answering honestly to all of the questions. A vampire only needs to carry for six months due to the aggressive rate of healing. Labor pains do occur but having someone use mind control on the mother will certainly ease her discomfort. Immortal babies do not feed off their mother but instead the mother will have to consume twice the amount of blood to avoid starvation of the baby.

Elise warned Grant that vampires can have twins like mortals and miscarry like mortals. Dr. Rowland told her to take it easy the next two months to ensure the baby was safe. Two major events would be occurring: their wedding and the Council visit but Elise must follow doctor orders if she wanted a healthy baby. Rest is what she needed for now. A lot of times vampires miscarry on their first pregnancy because the body tries to void the foreign tissue.

Due to the morning sickness Elise was having she had to inform the family right away so they didn't suspect a bad blood supply and then enforcers would go to the warehouse in frenzy. She dreaded telling her Uncle but he would just read her mind anyway and find out. Grant agreed to go to her Uncle with her and take any lashing he gave. They found him in his office reading the newspaper quietly when they knocked on the door together. Almost instantly Roman sensed something different in the air and laid the newspaper down gently on his desk.

"What is it?" Roman asked.

"Uncle we've just come from Dr. Rowland's office and have the most wonderful news. We are going to have a baby." Elise said biting her lip as she waited for a reaction.

"Oh, this soon?" he asked as his eyebrows rose high on his forehead.

Elise slumped forward discouraged at her uncle's reaction. Grant read her mind and put his arm around her as if he would not let anyone's words or actions hurt her even if it was from family.

"Roman, think of this as you will but we are delighted to become parents and your blessing is not needed." Grant announced sternly as he looked Roman in the eye.

Realizing his words came out harshly Roman stood up and apologized for his behavior and hugged them both sharing in their happiness. He immediately sensed her ill feeling and temporarily took her off enforcement duty to rest before the wedding. This baby would be the most important immortal in all of history and he had to make sure Elise's son would be delivered safely into this world.

"Uncle, you had me worried. Are you truly excited for us?" Elise asked.

"Of course, now go tell the others. Go on..." he said as he showed them out of his office. They turned down the hall and set out to find Lucas, Santiago, Bart, and Veronica.

Roman quietly shut his office door and nervously paced back and forth. He had to inform the Council right away that what they had been expecting had arrived a year earlier. A new baby in the mansion brought so much joy however this baby was special and soon other immortals will find out and want to steal him. Roman could already get a reading on the tiny fetus growing in Elise's stomach and knew that it would be a boy and he would possess the most power any vampireire had ever seen.

Roman quickly picked up the phone and called the head Council member himself trying to whisper so nobody could hear him. He was going to have to hire more enforcers and watchmen for the gates without Grant and Elise realizing.

****

Everyone was thrilled with the news of having a sweet baby coming soon. Veronica jumped for joy as she hugged her friend. Lucas and Santiago high-fived Grant and patted him on the back. Bart gave Elise a hug only a brotherly role model could give and wished her nothing but the best.

Elise knew that from now on they would treat her like a fragile bird since most first pregnancies ended tragically but she was determined to do everything to keep her little love bug. She laughed at herself for giving the baby a nickname when she had just found out she was pregnant less than an hour ago.

Bart and Veronica were sitting close together and Elise suspected a romance in the works. She eyed Bart suspiciously with a devious smile on her face letting him know she knew of their connection. He smiled and sent a message to Elise saying he thinks he found the one. Elise tried to hold back her excitement so she didn't draw attention to their silent conversation.

Everyone took time away from their busy day to celebrate with Grant and Elise. They ordered in Elise's favorite food and a messenger retrieved Sky Chili for Grant. The evening turned out to be an action movie and food extravaganza while Roman stayed in his office on the phone with the Council until the early hours developing a strategy to protect his niece's unborn child. Elise sensed that her uncle was worried about something but he was blocking his thoughts. She sat among her friends and snuggled against her fiancée as they watched the movie but in the back of her mind she knew Uncle Roman was hiding something and it had to do with the news she just told them.

Four months would come quick and as soon as the wedding was over she would need to start interviewing immortal nanny's to keep an eye on her love bug when enforcing duty called. There was so much to do but she vowed not to get too stressed about it and preserve her energy for the sake of their baby. Grant was too involved in the movie to notice Elise's worries or thoughts. She decided she would confront her uncle the next day on his reaction to the pregnancy.

****

The next evening Grant and Elise woke up from much needed rest. They had stayed up late watching movies all day long. Grant cupped Elise's face in his hands and kissed her nose before he rose out of bed to shower. He needed to get to his office to see if the legal team approved the contracts for vehicles to be sent to a new client. She loved that he took pride in his work and chose to continue working even though he knew money would no longer be a problem.

The bed linens were so cool and crisp that it made it hard for her to want to get up. She was temporarily on leave from work which gave her extra time to focus on the last details for the wedding ceremony. Realizing how many little things needed done she sighed as she rolled out of bed to grab a bag of blood. She felt better this morning as if her body was adjusting to the new addition. She quickly put on some yoga pants and a t-shirt and decided she would visit her Uncle first.

****

"Elise, you're awake; good. The caterer called and asked if you would like individual wedding cakes for the guests or have the traditional huge wedding cake." Veronica asked as she was knee deep in wedding decorations.

"Whatever you think is fine with me. I'm not worried about cake just as long as I have my love by my side." She said with a wonderful glow.

Veronica smiled as that basically meant she could run wild with ideas. She quickly picked up the phone to call the caterer back as she tied ribbons on the flowers. Looking at the floor around Veronica you would have thought she bought out all the fabric and flower stores. Tulle, lace, and ribbon were everywhere. Surely she wasn't going to use all of it. Elise decided she would sneak out of the room to find her Uncle. She wanted answers and fast.

****

Elise found her Uncle in the main sitting room enjoying a glass of wine. She felt the twinge at her temples as his thoughts were overflowing with information. He seemed bothered by something and it involved her. She saw images of watchmen lined around the perimeter of the estate leaving no room for someone to slip through. They were armed with weapons used only on immortals and stood with eyes glowing.

"Uncle, what are the watchmen for? You must tell me immediately. Are we in danger?" Elise said abruptly realizing she had caught him off guard.

She daringly stepped in the room without permission to enter and stood in front of her Uncle demanding an answer. Staring in his deep purple eyes she tried to read his mind for more details but he instantly blocked her. He knew he had no right to keep important news from her especially when it regarded her unborn child. Reluctantly, he decided he could not hide the inevitable.

"Sit down and I will tell you everything. I'm telling you this not because you demanded it of me, but because it involves Grant, the baby, and you." He explained.

"Uncle, you are scaring me. I've never heard you speak of this way before."

"What we will experience in the next coming months has been something many Grand Vampire's before me have dreaded would come. A legend has been told for centuries in the ancient immortal prophecy books and the time has come where we must defend what's coming. Although it will be a scary time for you, I need you to understand what will happen and why."

Elise was drawn in by her Uncle's words and trusted him for he was the Grand Vampire of the world. She nodded and remained silent so he would continue. He placed his hand on the seat next to him as a sign for her to sit.

"First of all, I want to inform you that the Council chose Grant to become immortal because his destiny is to take over my position when my responsibility retires. Your future husband is going to be the next Grand Vampire." He said as he watched her eyes carefully for emotion.

Elise knew that Grant was different and that the Council had chosen him for something big but had no clue that it was because he would be prepped to rule all the immortals in the world. She was very pleased with the Council's decision and believed Grant would succeed. However, she assumed that Grant did not know he would be expected to assume that role in the future.

"You are correct in the fact that Grant does not know he is the next Grand Vampire. Only the Council and I know and now you my dear niece. I figured when he was fully adapted in his new lifestyle I would have the conversation with him. However, given the recent turn of events that is not the priority of my concern any longer."

There was more she thought? Elise didn't know if she would be able to hear so much life changing news in one day. She was already trying to get used to being the future Mrs. Grand Vampire and now she had a feeling the next news would not be so pleasant. Sensing her concern, Roman rose from the high backed chair to pour her a glass of warm blood hoping it would bring ease. He knew his next statement would bring much alarm and he grew nervous by every passing second that he nearly knocked over the glass goblet. He quickly corrected his clumsiness as he would need to be strong for his niece.

"Elise, I have watched you grow into a fine mortal and then assisted you when you were violently turned to immortality. Nothing gives me more pleasure than seeing you marry your life mate. I also know you will be a wonderful Mother to your Son." Roman said as he smiled giving her the gender of the baby.

"Uncle, your intuition tells you we are going to have a baby boy?" she asks excitedly.

Roman shakes his head yes as she hugs him and could not wait to find Grant to tell him the news. Thinking the discussion was over, she turned to head out the door when her Uncle stopped her and said there was more she must know. She turned to face her Uncle and walked back to the seat she just left.

"When you came to my office and invaded my thoughts, the images you saw were correct. The Cantonelli estate is officially on lockdown by orders of the Council until further notice. Extra enforcers from around the world are actively making their way here and near city limits to ensure safety."

"I don't understand. Who exactly is the army of enforcers keeping safe?"

"You." Roman said with his head bowed unable to look at her.

"Me? Oh that's absurd. Why would I be in danger? After all, the immortal that attacked me was turned to dust."

"Elise before I say anything further it is probably best to have Grant here with you." Roman said as he silently beckoned Grant to his office.

Moments later there was a knock on the door. With a wave of his hand Roman opened it and Grant stood there waiting for permission to enter.

"I received your message. Is everything okay here?" he asked as he studied Elise for an answer.

Before Elise could speak, Roman stood and ordered Grant to take his chair next to Elise while he paced back and forth. Grant felt that Roman had troubling news and was having a hard time expressing it. Roman looked at Grant and nodded his head yes confirming his feeling.

Grant grabbed Elise's left hand and placed it on his knee rubbing it back and forth trying to soothe her anxiety. Or was it to soothe his? He smiled at his soon to be wife to show some positivity and then eyeballed Roman until he finally was able to explain what was going on.

"I first want to start off by explaining to Grant why the Council chose him to become immortal. As you know I hold a high power of being the Grand Vampire for all immortals in the world. That position will be passed down in ten years for the next immortal to rule. The Council chooses the lucky immortal based on personality, work ethic, love for others, love for this planet, and so on. This time a mortal was chosen which has never happened before until now. Grant, you were given immortality from the Council in the expectation that you will be the next Grand Vampire."

CHAPTER FIFTEEN

Grant sat motionless with his mouth wide open in shock of what he just heard. Roman went into detail of the responsibilities a Grand Vampire is tasked with and his head was swimming with emotion. Elise looked at her husband admirably as she held his hands tight waiting for his response. She knew this was a shock to him and he would have questions but with her Uncle's help he would be the greatest Grand Vampire immortals have ever seen.

"What if I reject this plan for my future?" Grant asked, eyeing Roman daringly.

Elise's back straightened at his question and looked at her Uncle with pleading eyes to spare him of lashing. Although Roman wanted to catapult him to the next country after disgracing such a calling of high power, he was also reminded that Grant was just getting used to his new lifestyle and did not know that rejecting the Council's plans meant imminent death.

"The only remnants of your body would be dust to the wind: If I make myself clear?" Roman huffed.

"Grant I know you are in shock but you wouldn't be Grand Vampire for another ten years. I'm sure Uncle will train you in the necessary protocols and you will always have my full support, darling." Elise explained.

Grant looked at Roman for confirmation of Elise's words and he nodded agreeing of her statement.

"I understand this is a lot for you to take in just becoming a part of the family. I assure you training and skills you will need to achieve this position will be taught by me and if I am not capable, then the Council. However, this is not the main topic of conversation I asked you to come for, Grant."

"There is more, really?" he said exasperatingly.

"Unfortunately and it is not to be taken lightly." Roman said glaring.

****

Lucas and Santiago was notified by the watchmen at the gate of two approaching vehicles. They were not aware of any visitors scheduled and brought the gate image up on the full screen in the conference room watching as the imposters were being interrogated. Occasionally, mortals would get lost trying to find the golf club that was located on the other side of town. With its massive, green rolling hills, the estate had the illusion of being a golf course.

"Sir, the visitors say they are enforcers from Germany hired by Roman Cantonelli. Should I allow them entry?" a watchman announced over the radio.

Lucas and Santiago looked at each other perplexed as they were not aware of more enforcers being hired. Surely, Roman would have told them.

"Sir, ten more vehicles of enforcers have also arrived. What do you want us to do?" the watchman said.

"Please allow them entry. I will notify Roman of their arrival." Santiago said.

They turned the screen off and made their way to Roman's office when they heard shouting on the other side of his door. Someone is not happy, they thought.

Santiago pointed at Lucas and motioned for him to knock on the door.

"What is it?" Roman yelled.

Lucas opened the door and announced the arrival of enforcers and asked where they should be kept until Roman was ready for them.

"Put them in the conference room, Lucas, and then gather every staff member for a meeting in the library." Roman announced.

Lucas agreed and shut the office door.

"Something is going on, Santiago. Go alert Bartholomew and Veronica. I'll usher the guests to the conference room." Lucas said.

****

"So you mean to tell us that our unborn Son will have the power to facilitate an immense love and peace to those who are destined?" Elise asked her Uncle in awe.

"It has been a legend until now and per the ancient prophecy scroll, the son of a Grand Vampire who was once mortal will behold the power for immortals and mortals to love one another for who they are. The Rogue vampires will see your son as a threat to their existence and try everything in their power for him not to be born. As you know Rogues thrive on inflicting pain and your son's gift could change the world against them.

Elise broke into tears as she paced the floor with her face planted in her hands. Grant looked at Roman in disbelief but then saw the single tear roll down his cheek, fall and then absorb into the carpet. He then knew that Roman was telling the truth and that their son's life was in danger. He hugged his fiancée and whispered assurances in her ear as he rubbed her back and let her cry. The future Grand

Vampire felt helpless against the rising evil that would try to take his new family away.

"Please help us. I will do anything." Grant pleaded to Roman with tearful eyes.

"I promise you I will protect Elise and the baby even if I become dust trying." Roman said with fiery eyes and determination of a powerful Grand Vampire.

Roman wiped the moisture from his cheek and like lightning left the room to begin preparations with the enforcers.

"Grant what are we going to do? We can't let anything happen to our son." Elise said with a shaken voice.

Grant realized the severity of the situation however he was not going to show his fears to his future bride. He knew that Roman and the enforcers would arrange the best plan of protection. His main goal was keeping Elise calm and the baby safe in the womb. He held Elise's face in his hands and kissed her nose thinking of how much happiness she has brought him. There was no way he was losing it all now.

"Darling, I am confident that Roman and the enforcers are making plans as we speak to ensure love bugs safety. I know for a fact that everything will play out perfectly and if I recall we have a certain event coming up that needs the final touches. Oh, what was it? I can't remember?" Grant talked coolly.

"How can we even pull a wedding off with the tight security and potential threats coming our way? "She said in distraught.

"Elise, I'm a successful businessman that does not back down from challenges. You are a beautiful, stubborn, immortal whom I've fallen in love with and I will not rest until our vows are heard in front of family, friends, and the Council."

Grant knew just how to put her mind at ease and he bent down slowly savoring the moment by kissing her passionately. Elise opened her mouth inviting him to explore with his tongue. She moaned as he wrapped his arm around her waist to pull her closer and spun her around, drawing her scarf to the side and softly kissed her neck. She could feel his tight chest muscles pressing against her back creating a stir in her lower belly.

"As much as I'd love to kiss you all day I don't think my Uncle would appreciate us christening his office. Plus, knowing him there are cameras hidden in the room." Elise said breathing heavily.

"You know how to ruin a mood, don't you darling?" Grant chuckled as he kissed her one last time.

"I have some XL business to take care of but when I'm through I'll be joining the others in the conference discussing the lockdown.

"I'm going to the sound booth to record some music for my album. I need to exercise my vocal chords to sing a certain song that is my lover's favorite at the weding." She said playfully biting his ear.

"Now, don't start things you are not able to finish my love. Go have therapy with music and I'll deal with preparations for our new "adventure". Grant said confidently.

Elise opened the office door with a wave of her hand then blew a kiss to Grant as they departed ways. He was worried sick about how he was going to keep her and the baby safe from Rogue vampires set out to destroy his family. He ran his fingers through his hair in desperation as he paced back and forth in the empty office. His mind ran rapid as he recalled the information he received from Roman today.

Gazing up at the enormously framed oil canvas hanging above the fireplace, he realized that it was Roman in his younger years. The painting was surely out of date and looked like it should be in a museum. Roman's glowing eyes were portrayed with fierceness as he lifted a sword into the air showing dominance to the obedient army below him. The army of purple eyed immortals looking at their new Grand Vampire with the moonlight shining on the land around them.

"I hope you can be our son's savior." Grant thought.

CHAPTER SIXTEEN

Months had passed and it was the day before Council was set to arrive to meet Grant and perform the wedding ceremony. Tension was high in the Cantonelli estate as preparations were complete and staff was on high alert. By 5 o'clock in the evening there was a total of seventy enforcers that offered their services to help defeat any Rogues that decided to show their ugly faces. Once they were screened by the gate watchmen and passed the routine mind reading protocol to ensure they were on the good side of the fight, Bartholomew and Veronica showed them to their rooms.

In all, the mansion held eighty one rooms in which sixty of them were bedrooms. For security purposes Roman thought the enforcers' rooms should be spread about the mansion to establish a well-balanced perimeter guard. The rooms for the six Council members would be located on the highest level of the mansion to keep them the farthest away from any danger. Lucas and Santiago thought it was wise to move

Grant and Elise's bedroom to the lowest level to create numerous barriers against Rogues if the mansion came under attack. In an emergency she would be locked into a steel cell until enforcers could stabilize the area. Of course Lucas hadn't mentioned that fact to her when everyone was invited to the mandatory meeting in the conference room.

Kieron was invited to the wedding but chose to stay home to be the eyes of the Northern hemisphere to monitor the rise of growing clusters of Rogues. The amount of equipment he would need to travel with him was too much to unload when the simplest strategy would be to stay home and watch the wedding via FangTime. Roman reluctantly agreed that Kieron remaining in Toronto would be the smartest surveillance plan and offered to ship him his own personal wedding meal prepared by the chefs.

****

The wedding ceremony was set up to take place in the ballroom followed by a toasting of warmed blood and hors d'oeuvres. Roman had hired the five top immortal chefs in North America to oversee the menu and kitchen staff. A band was hired to play music after dinner to serenade the guests into the wee hours of the morning. Santiago made sure extra blood supply was flown in from the warehouse to accommodate the guests, Council, enforcers, and to prepare for any injured vampires during an impending attack.

Cool Water Purple roses were chosen by Grant as their official wedding flower specifically as he would never forget the day he saw

Elise's beautiful purple glowing eyes. They decided on Purple and Red as their wedding colors. Red represented the blood immortals needed to continue their existence and to signify the night they tasted each other's blood for the first time during their time of intimacy.

Veronica was in the spare room double checking her floor setup for tables and chairs for the reception when Elise entered the room and she felt the awful twinge at her temples. It was apparent that Veronica was a perfectionist and wanted the night's events to transition smoothly. First on the agenda is the formal announcement of Mr. and Mrs. Grant Biltmore followed by a champagne toast. Of course the staff would have the flutes prepared prior to guest arrival. Next the band would play a light melody while guests mingled, enjoyed the food arrangement, and congratulated the new couple. This would give security the extra time to do a head count, take a photo of each guest discreetly for surveillance purposes and run them through the Rogue database, and report any findings to Roman.

If all checked out well the band would take stage and get everyone moving and having a wonderful time. Promptly at midnight the Council is scheduled to say a few words and perform the Chalices of Blood Unity for the newlyweds that has been passed down for centuries. A passage would then be read from the ancient scrolls written by the first generation Council in honor of immortality.

Last on the list is the cutting of the cake which is so typical of mortal weddings but Elise really wanted to capture some of the original mortal party traditions. Veronica began to wonder if Grant would smash cake in Elise's face like mortals did at receptions. She chuckled at the thought and continued on her event checklist.

Elise was able to hear the whole nights plan just in the few minutes of reading her mind and felt pleased with Veronica's work. It was one less thing she had to worry about since finding out about the threat against love bug. She couldn't wait to marry Grant but at the same time she had an awful feeling deep within her that something bad would happen during what is supposed to be their happily ever after. Most importantly she feared for her unborn baby's life and how others would view his powers. As a protective mother she rubbed her swollen stomach.

It must be the pregnancy hormones that caused the tears to well up in her eyes and of course Bart just happened to be walking through the hall and found her crying.

"Elise, what's wrong? Are you feeling alright?" Bart asked concerned.

"Oh Bart, I've never been happier." She said wiping her flowing tears.

"Then why the tears baby girl?" he asked.

"Have you ever thought about having children in a world that is so closed minded and afraid of change?" she asked.

"Elise, if you are wondering if bringing a child into this world is a good thing I would say definitely yes. After all, I hear your son is exactly what this world needs. The hatred and unhappiness that consumes this planet is overbearing and I've watched many mortals die without seeing the pleasantries of life. Your son is the window to change and the breath of fresh air so to speak."

Elise laid her head on Bart's shoulder smiling as his words were always helpful to her. She was glad that her son would have Bart to also lean to. A realization came to her that she needed to tend to right away. Every immortal child had a Guardian assigned to them at birth and Bartholomew would be the best person for the job. She thanked Bart for the talk and quickly made her way to Grant's office to speak to him about the tradition and to see if he agreed with her decision.

****

"Elise, darling what is the matter? Have you been crying?" Grant asked and immediately approached her.

"I just had a wonderful conversation with Bart about things and I wanted to get your opinion on something. At birth, every immortal child has a Guardian assigned to them to serve as their protector until the child needs them no more. I love Bart as if he is my brother and would like to appoint him as our son's guardian.

"I trust Bartholomew and believe you picked the right person for the job. However I worry that our son's unique gift will make his guardian position very difficult." He said with a smile.

Elise chuckled and agreed that no matter what they will have their hands full but they felt honored to be parents of a legend told in ancient sacred books. Not one immortal in the world will possess the gift their son will have. When the Council arrived she wanted to ask them why and how they were chosen.

"On another note I was thinking about where to take you for our honeymoon and realized that my pregnant wife may not be up for traveling far and having the extra security following our every move wouldn't be that much fun. So your uncle helped me arrange a special surprise."

"Darling, wherever you are is where I want to be. I have my life mate and soon will experience motherhood. I already have the best present."

Grant's eyes began to glow as her words created a stir in him that made him crave her in every way. He wanted to scoop her in his arms and carry her to their bedroom and kiss every inch of her body until she begged him to stop. She could hear his thoughts and boldly stared him in his eyes as if daring him to make it happen. Grant was amused in her playful demeanor and instead of carrying her out of the room he chose to take her there in his office. With a motion of his hand his office door closed and locked itself and then he silently ordered his desk to clear. The files, mail, and pens that were so neatly placed on his desk floated to the floor in an organized fashion. Arousal coursed through her body as she watched her fiancée show off his newly acquired mind control skills.

He took his shirt off and folded it under her head to act as a cushion while he laid her down tasting her most intimate areas and rounded belly. She couldn't believe how much she loved that man and that he was all hers. Pulling him on top of her gently she kissed him hard on his lips as if she couldn't get enough. Sensing her readiness he entered her and they made passionate love until they both felt the pleasant rush of excitement.

****

CHAPTER SEVENTEEN

"OK people this is it. The Council and the selected honorary vampires have arrived and I'm sure are in need of refreshments. There are a total of six Council members so make sure they each get personalized attention. Luke, get the parlor chairs ready and blood warmed. Santiago, you will take their luggage to the assigned suites. Veronica, I need you to get Kieron access to the security mainframe so he has video going in every room. Bartholomew, find Grant and Elise and tell them to come to the parlor room. Oh Bartholomew, make sure you knock first." Roman declared to all of his family as he made his way to greet the Council in the foyer.

Bart walked briskly down the hall toward Grant's office wondering why Roman made it clear to knock first. He reached the door with the name plate on it of XL Properties and grabbed the handle getting ready to twist it open when the door opened on its own. Elise was straightening up her skirt while Grant was tucking in his dress shirt as they tried to hide their mischievous grins from Bart. Elise had heard Bart's overpowering thoughts as he was stomping down the hallway and alerted Grant that company was coming to dress quickly.

Bart's face turned many shades of red as he now understood why Roman said to knock first. It seemed the happy couple was in the middle of doing "happy" things. He told them of the Council's arrival and that they were requested to the parlor immediately.

"Are you ready to meet the Council?" Elise asked Grant nervously.

"I am but I have been wondering why everyone treats them like royalty. I mean your uncle is the Grand Vampire, not them." Grant reasoned.

"Think of them as the Congress over immortals, and Roman as the President. You do not want to be on their bad side." Bart replied.

****

"Greetings, Roman! How are you old friend?" Creighton, the eldest of the Council asked as he shook Roman's hand.

"I am well. I hope your travel was comfortable?" Roman asked.

"Indeed. We traveled in style and luxury thanks to Mr. Biltmore's auto company. I think I may need to purchase one for my better half at home. She would have something to talk about amongst her friends during her tea parties." Creighton said happily.

"That can be arranged. Creighton you have seen my enforcers via camera but I'd like to personally introduce you to the Cantonelli crew. This is Lucas, Santiago, Veronica, and Bartholomew. If you need anything during your stay you find one of them if I'm unavailable. Kieron is also available via FangTime from Canada as he is always our digital eyes and ears globally," Roman said.

Creighton stepped further into the parlor as he shook hands with each immortal and performed a quick mind read. It was policy for every Council member to screen every immortal they come into physical contact with just in case they are connected to someone who wrote the prophecy scrolls. If a person was a descendant of the original scribers they would be forever cherished and given a title of Counselor of Valor. Only five have been discovered in the world.

The remaining members of the Council followed behind Creighton introducing themselves to all of the enforcers and then corralled around the goblets filled with warm blood. Roman was pleased with how well everything was going so far. He received an update from the gate watchmen that no Rogues had been spotted in the area and he began to relax a little.

Mini conversations filled the room as everyone got to know each other better when Grant and Elise entered the room hand in hand. Silence filled the room as the Council turned to face the next Grand Vampire. Grant felt a rush of embarrassment as many purple eyes were focused on him in adoration.

"Members of the Council, I'm honored to introduce you to Mr. Grant Biltmore, the next Grand Vampire of all immortals." Roman announced with pride.

Creighton, the lead Council member began clapping which led everyone in the room to join in the roar of applause. The enforcers and even Roman were clapping and it made Grant feel unworthy. He didn't understand why he was receiving such praise when he hadn't done anything yet. Creighton read Grant's thoughts, stopped clapping and stepped forward and reached for his hand. The room became quiet to hear the Council speak.

"Grand Vampire is a high honor that was only given to immortals of great leadership qualities. For the first time in history was a mortal chosen and turned just for this task. Embrace the journey that was given to you; for you Grant Biltmore will pave the future for all vampires." Creighton explained with pride.

Grant smiled as the words boosted his confidence. He was able to relax a little and enjoyed the rest of the night in conversation with the Council and the other vampires from around the world who were brought in to honor him as if he was a natural Grand Vampire.

****

The next day, Elise laid in her bed to rest before the big day tomorrow and had her laptop resting on top of her legs. She missed Grant and an idea crossed her mind. Hitting compose in her email inbox she sent her future husband an email. A telepathic message could have easily been sent to him but she thought an email would be more romantic and they could print them out for their scrapbook. Grant always had his phone by his side for emergencies with his auto business. A ping for every email received and then that annoying blinking light for notification always made Grant feel like he needed to read it right away so the light would stop.

He was probably sitting at his desk hunched over his computer typing while music playing softly on the surround sound Santiago had installed for him.

To: GBiltmoreXL@XL.com

From: Cantonelli.Elise@vmail.com

Date: November 16, 2014 3:30 am EST

Subject: Becoming Mrs. Biltmore

We aren't supposed to see each other until the wedding so I thought an electronic message would not be breaking the rules

As love bug and I rest in bed I can't help but miss you lying next to me. I never thought I would find a life mate and most of all him turn out to be the future Grand Vampire. I guess that would make me Mrs. Grand Vampire?

I suspect you are working or did the guys capture you for a drink?

Love,

Elise Cantonelli almost Biltmore

To: Cantonelli.Elise@vmail.com
From: GBiltmoreXL@XL.com
Date: November 16, 2014 3:34 am EST
Subject: Lonely in Love

I am glad to hear you are resting and yes I'm working in my office. It seems that Creighton has ordered luxury vehicles for every Council member and one for his wife. Lucas and Santiago did persuade me into an alcoholic beverage earlier however it made me feel weird. I didn't think you would like a drunken groom for your dream wedding.

Don't stay up too late. I plan on tiring you out tomorrow.

Love,
Grant Biltmore future Grand Vampire

****

"Elise, time to wake up! The hairdresser and makeup artist are here. It is beauty time." Veronica said excitedly as she pulled back the blankets covering Elise.

"Oh, no. What time is it? Am I late?" Elise said half asleep as she rubbed her eyes.

After Grant's email last night she powered down her laptop and consumed two bags of blood before turning in for the night. She had a wonderful dream about two vampires getting married and then it quickly turned into a nightmare when Rogues snatched love bug out of her arms and threw him over a fiery cliff. She woke up crying and distraught until she realized it was not reality and then must have drifted back asleep.

Veronica heard her thoughts and suggested a warm bath might make her feel better. She had also brought her a goblet of warmed blood to help ease her morning sickness. Veronica made Elise's bed while she was in the bathroom soaking in bubbles. She also placed some yoga pants and a large t-shirt on the bed for her to change into. Elise would get five star treatment including a massage, hair and makeup detail, and then Veronica would help her into her lavish wedding gown.

"I'm going downstairs to entertain your beauty entourage. Take your time and relax. I placed your clothes on the bed when you are ready for pampering." Veronica yelled out to Elise from behind the bathroom door.

"Thank you, Veronica. I won't be too long. Say, have you seen Grant up and about?" Elise asked.

"I just saw him in the hallway talking to Roman. It looked like they were both in the best of spirits." Veronica replied.

What are those two up to she wondered.

Elise soaked her pregnant body in the purple bubbles and rubbed her hands over her protruding belly that grew larger every day. Finding clothes that fit her became a challenge and had to send someone out once a week to purchase a larger size. She rested her head on the back of the tub and closed her eyes thinking about her soon to be magical day.

Chapter Eighteen

The ballroom was elegantly decorated while the lighting was dimmed to give the room a more romantic appeal. It's high ceiling windows were draped with red curtains and tall purple pillar candles were placed in all the window sills. On the left side of the ballroom, rows and rows of white chairs with purple bows were filled as the orchestra played a soft melody in the background. A red carpet was laid out over the flooring of the ballroom for Elise's grand entrance. On the right side of the room, tall bar tables and chairs were set up for the reception that was to immediately follow the ceremony. Veronica had gotten Roman's approval of the layout for security reasons and Roman confirmed the windows were bulletproof.

The staff, chefs, enforcers that came from all over the world, Council, Cantonelli enforcers, and Dr. Rowland were all in attendance. Grant realized that Dr. Rowland was the only mortal from his past and welcomed his new friend to witness their vows.

Grant and Elise were not fond of having a big wedding but they were grateful to the enforcers who traveled and volunteered their time to keep Elise and the baby safe.

Roman stood at the farthest end of the room wearing his elaborate Grand Vampire robe for formal occasions as he held the ancient immortal book of vows. Grant stood to the left of Roman dressed in contemporary white tux and black cummerbund. He never thought he would be the marrying kind but it just goes to show how everything can change in a blink of an eye. His attack in the chili parlor bathroom was horrific but at the same time it gave him a chance to really live.

Grant had asked Santiago to be his best man since they learned a lot about each other after Grant's turn. Their friendship had become something they both valued. As Santiago stood to the left of Grant in a black tux he was grinning ear to ear imagining how his wedding would be. Grant heard his thoughts and sent him a telepathic message teasing him about his high girlfriend turnover rate and that the Council would have to order him to get married. Santiago chuckled out loud and quickly tried to cover his slip with a stoned face as Roman glared at him angrily. Grant smiled at the fact that his message got Santiago in trouble.

The orchestra began to play an upbeat instrumental song and everyone looked toward the back of the room. Grant waited for the cherry wood double doors to open in anticipation and after several seconds of no activity he began to worry when he received a message from Elise saying she had just gotten sick moments prior and Veronica was reapplying her lipstick for her. Roman looked at Grant in concern when Grant leaned over to whisper in his ear the message Elise had sent him. Roman nodded his head that he understood and made a frown face to show he felt sorry that happened just before her walk down the aisle.

At the second time of the orchestra playing the song the doors finally opened and Veronica made her way down the aisle with a large goblet of blood that was passed down from the first ever immortal wedding in the Cantonelli family. It was pure gold with a large C engraved in the middle. The stem and base of the goblet was adorned with shining diamonds the size of a pencil eraser. She wore a form fitting strapless lace red dress with long flowing silk ruffles at the knees which grew longer in the back and sported a small train. The purple gem necklace she wore looked radiant against her tanned skin as she held her arms high holding the ancient goblet with care. She passed Bartholomew sitting in the crowd and winked at him which made his eyes glow in arousal. Placing the goblet gently on the round pedestal in front of Roman, Veronica took her place as Maid of Honor.

The "Here Comes the Bride" song began to play and all of the guests stood up in honor of Elise. She held a beautiful arrangement of red and purple roses at her waist to help hide her small bump that seemed to have grown overnight. Stepping forward into the light of the overhead chandeliers she looked breathtaking and Grant thought so too as she noticed his glowing eyes. Deciding her hair was just too short to do anything with, her hairdresser suggested extensions that give her a voluptuous look. Blonde bouncing curls danced around her Barbie doll painted face as she walked slowly. Her strapless white dress clung to her swollen breasts as her skin glistened from her massage earlier and iridescent lotion used. Her dress was made from satin, silk, and lace which hugged her frame perfectly until halfway below her knee the dress formed into a lace and gold embellished long train.

She smiled as she walked past the rows of chairs filled with guests never taking her eyes off Grant. As a woman it was the best feeling in the world to feel beautiful and confident as she finally reached the end of the aisle and locked arms with Grant and then handed her bouquet of flowers to Veronica. The orchestra stopped playing and everyone turned their gaze to the front of the room. She smiled lovingly at her uncle and then suddenly her stomach contents began to flip flop and she felt ill again. She gripped Grant underneath his arm to balance herself when suddenly her sickness went away and she was well again. In confusion she looked up at Grant for an explanation when he looked in Santiago's direction and saw his glowing eyes in a trance. Santiago had heard her thoughts about being ill and decided to give her temporary relief until the ceremony ended. She smiled and sent a thank you message telepathically.

"As we all gather here today in honor of Grant and Elise we must remember this night for centuries to come. We will begin the ceremony with the traditional drinking of the goblet to honor and remember our ancestors who have made us who we are today." Roman declared.

Roman lifted the goblet from the pedestal and gave it to Grant ordering him to drink and then pass to Elise to finish off. This act is to symbolize the unity of two immortals becoming one for all of eternity until dust do them part. Elise tilted the glass to drink the remaining blood and placed the goblet back on the pedestal. She hoped Santiago's mind control would help her keep it down at least until after the wedding. Blood is so hard to get out of a white dress.

Since the guests in the room were immortal they knew that Elise was fighting from morning sickness and that Santiago was easing her discomfort. It was so hard to keep secrets from other immortals unless thoughts were guarded. However with Elise's sickness and the fact she was in the process of getting married she was not able to focus hard enough to guard them.

"Love is a powerful feeling that every culture, generation, mortal, and immortal has experienced at some point in their lifetime. It is the one thing that binds us together and is easiest to understand. Though for some immortals finding their life mate never happens but if fate gives you the opportunity, seize it. It is an honor to stand before you not only as Grand Vampire but as Uncle to Elise Cantonelli and I approve the marriage of the two immortals that stand before me. Since their decision to unite was consummated a while ago there will not be contests from others and the vampire clause of loyalty to

ANGEL MUSK

one another shall be in place for all of eternity or until dust do them part." Roman dutifully stated.

Grant and Elise were now face to face and he could see happy tears filling her eyes as she heard her uncle speak. He grabbed her hands and held them in preparation for the vow exchanges coming up. They each had chosen to write their own vows on ancient papyrus scrolls to be sealed in a time capsule that would be opened in one hundred years.

"Grant will begin with the vows he has written and Elise will follow after him." Roman said.

"The first moment I saw you I wanted to get to know you better. Even though you had abducted me and was holding me captive, I fell in love. This is the first day of our lives together officially as one and I can't wait to see our beautiful baby that we made together" Grant said as he read from his scroll.

Grant handed the scroll to Creighton and Elise opened her scroll nervously. Grant smiled at her as she fumbled with unlocking it to extend.

"I was not prepared to fall in love with my assignment, but I'm so glad to have found an eternal companion. I hope to be the best life mate for you and mother to our child. I will support you in every way and be by your side when you become Grand Vampire." Elise said as she stared in Grant's eyes.

As Elise handed her scroll to Creighton to be locked and sealed immediately, she noticed that Grant was staring at her with an evil expression. His eyes were glassy looking, squinted and eyebrows bunched together and down. It sent a chill down her spine.

"Grant, are you okay?" she asked.

Elise's tone alerted Roman to look at Grant and immediately he rushed into action. He read his mind and was stunned to find out the horror he was about to unleash.

"Enforcer's, Code Shadow! Initiate protective measures!" Roman yelled to everyone in the room.

He looked at his beautiful niece with tears in his eyes and sent her a message that the blood in the goblet Grant partook of was charmed with a spell. However, she too had been infected and the baby was in danger.

"Dr. Rowland, get Elise to the hospital now and perform a body scan promptly" Roman commanded as he threw the chalice of blood in the fireplace.

Elise dropped her bouquet to the floor in horror as she was whisked away by enforcers. She watched as five enforcers struggled Grant to the floor. Her wedding had just turned into a nightmare and now her fears were coming true as love bug was in danger. Roman cancelled the rest of the ceremony due to the situation however Grant and Elise were still considered officially married even though Grant didn't get to kiss his bride.

****

"How in the hell did this happen" Roman shouted to his team of enforcers as he paced back and forth in the conference room.

It had been twenty minutes since the charm was discovered and every enforcer was given a task. The live feed on the internet and TV was turned off. The Vampire Council had been escorted to a secured suite until the situation could be fully assessed. Grant had been taken to a steel cell so he could not harm anyone while under the influence of the charm. All of the honorary guests were shown to their rooms for the night after having their rooms checked for intruders or anything out of the ordinary. They were ordered by the Vampire Council not to speak about the incident with any family or friends until the situation was dissolved. If word spread that the future Grand Vampire was charmed it would give the illusion that he would be incompetent to lead. The hired staff brought in for the wedding had their minds read for any crimes or ill will and were released to go home after being sworn to secrecy.

"Sir, we screened all hired staff that walked through the door and then some. Someone had to have seen something" Bartholomew said addressing the entire room in desperation. He had to get his emotions controlled but his worry for Elise and the baby was overpowering.

Veronica stood next to him rubbing his back trying to ease his concern and show support.

One of the enforcers from Brazil stood up reluctantly and began speaking, however it was in Portuguese. Roman turned towards the woman and listened to her intently as he knew thirteen different languages. Bart tried to comprehend but he was not as old as Roman and did not have the experience of learning other cultures yet. He saw the woman lower her arm to the floor as if explaining something small then became visibly upset and began speaking faster until she buried her hands in her face crying.

"Roman, what is she saying?" asked Bartholomew.

"The only clue we have at the moment. Consuela said she was guarding the garden terrace when a gray kitten, possibly a stray, wandered up to her. She knelt down to pet it for a couple of seconds then scooped it up and opened the iron gate to put it back behind the stone wall. She estimates the terrace was not guarded for approximately a minute and a half. Long enough for a Rogue vampire to swiftly gain entry and put a charm on the blood destined for Grant and Elise. Whoever it was knew of the wedding today and the traditional immortal ceremony procedures." Roman said as he addressed the room of enforcers he had hired to avoid this situation.

His anger was imminent and every enforcer was ashamed of letting the Grand Vampire down. They had never felt more inferior knowing that this happened all because of a blasted cat. A highly trained enforcer should not have let the distraction take her away from her duty.

****

Santiago stood outside the cell door watching Grant as he sat on the floor showing no emotion as if he was a robot. The charm would not present itself because he was not physically near Elise anymore. Until they were reunited, he could be in a conscious but paralyzed state. Santiago saw those types of charms before and in his experience the charms did not go away until the specified mission was completed. The question remaining is, what did the charm want Grant to do to Elise and the baby. Then Santiago shook his head in disbelief as he had a clue. He quickly radioed to all enforcers and to Roman.

"Santiago here. I have reason to believe the creator of the charm picked Grant to kill the unborn baby. They didn't have any other way of doing it themselves so they chose someone on the inside, closest to Elise and less expecting to carry out the mission. It is imperative that we keep Grant away from Elise. The charm is not active unless it senses Elise in close proximity to Grant." He explained diligently.

Lucas replied back, "Confirmed." As he looked at Roman in despair as they both realized the charm could be longer lasting than what they had suspected. It was not going away until the future Grand Vampire's offspring was eliminated.

Roman then turned to Consuela and commanded her to be escorted off the property and revoked her enforcer status banning her from any future work with the Cantonelli family. She was dishonorably discharged and would be put on a plane back to her country. He said it in Portuguese for her to understand and then in English so the other enforcers who did not know the language could hear his command and punishment. Clearly, he used Consuela as an example of his wrath if any other enforcer failed their duties.

"Sir, this is Kieron. May I interrupt?"

"What have you got for me, Kieron?" Roman said as turned toward the video screen.

"I was able to pull the satellite images of the estate from the last couple days and discovered a possible lead. I'm bringing up an image on the screen of a suspect who was in the garden terrace that Consuela was patrolling this morning. If you watch the footage from the time of 6:03 to 6:04 you will see a three second blur of motion around the same time the kitten was spotted. The animal was clearly a distraction for the intruder to gain entry," Kieron said.

As Kieron brought up the images on the screen every enforcer studied the footage diligently for any other possible information. So far, Kieron's theory seemed to be correct however the intruder's identity needed to be revealed.

"Hello Kieron, Veronica here. Were you able to get a good image of the intruder to tell if we are looking for a male or female?"

"I am working on slowing down the video in order to get a high resolution image. Once I have the intruders face I will be sure to alert all of you." Kieron said and then signed off to begin his work.

As the FangTime screen turned black and Kieron's signal was gone all the enforcers looked at Roman who was sitting at the head of the conference table. His head bowed in a feeling of defeat and in denial that this could be happening. Not only was his niece's life and baby in jeopardy, a family member under a charm, vampires chosen to be awarded for their generosity and was hosting the Vampire Council in his home, he also had a team of enforcers to lead and motivate to conquer the immortal war beginning. He had handled stressful times well in the past which is why the Vampire Council anointed him as Grand Vampire, however this was all happening too close to home. He blocked his recent thoughts from all immortals so they did not see his vulnerability and raised his head only to realize his team had been staring at him waiting for orders. Their determined faces and eagerness to fight the enemy gave him an abundance of strength and confidence which led to the next phase of orders.

"Does anyone have any ideas or concerns that need to be addressed?" Roman asked wearily.

"Sir, I just want you to know that we will not rest until our family is out of danger. I'm sure I speak for the whole table that we will fight to our deaths to keep everyone safe." Lucas said with his voice strained from emotion.

"Santiago here, sir. I wanted to let you know that there is no change in Grant and I await your further orders." As he radioed from the walkie talkie.

Roman sat with his hands clasped together on top of the table as he listened then unleashed the next plan of attack which left them all wide-eyed as they peered around the room studying each other's reactions.

****

Dr. Rowland was busy in his lab analyzing the samples he had taken from Elise. He dropped the blood on a slide and placed it underneath the microscope. As he suspected the charm was affixed to each blood cell however the good news was that the charm was not self-multiplying. What worried him was not knowing what the charm was doing to the unborn child. He looked across the room at Elise sleeping in the hospital bed trying to think of his next plan of treatment. He had never had a patient that was immortal, pregnant, and under the influence of a charm.

Roman entered the lab and saw Dr. Rowland assessing his niece and her swollen pouch. He knocked on the door and asked to enter.

"Mr. Cantonelli, I am doing my very best to treat her. She is unconscious but is responding when spoken to. It's like she's trapped in her own body but cannot speak or open her eyes. I do not have experience with treating charm victims, sir." Dr. Rowland said with fear and sorrow.

"I know you are, Dr. Rowland and I hear your concern. Would it be helpful to fly in another doctor to assist you? Roman asked.

"That would be recommended if you are able to do that. I would also suggest an OB/GYN to help monitor the baby," the doctor said.

"I can do anything Dr. Rowland, remember that," Roman said in a voice of threat as he walked around the bed staring at his beautiful niece.

"Look, sir, you have nothing to worry about with me. I know my history of attacking immortals is still vibrant in your memories however I am just as worried about Elise as you are. Maybe one day you will consider me family as well", Dr. Rowland admitted then returned to his lab.

Roman felt thankful a doctor was here, but was not convinced that Elise was in the best of care. He kissed Elise on her forehead. Elise could feel her uncle's touch and reached out to him grasping his arm.

"What do you need my sweet?" he asked as he brushed her cheek with his finger.

She let out a whimper and a solid flowing tear from her eyes fell down her cheek, wetting his finger. Bombarded with emotions he fled the room at once to initiate the immediate flights of several immortal doctors from around the world. The doctors would know that an order coming from the Grand Vampire was mandatory and had no choice to refuse.

CHAPTER NINETEEN

In Grant's cell there was a small bed and a refrigerator supplied with blood. The room was dark with a red heat lamp installed in the ceiling. He looked around the room and discovered himself sitting on the floor with his shoes off. *Where the hell was he now?* He stood up but quickly realized he was not well. He was dizzy and his head pounded like something fierce so he sat back down to try and compose himself. The temperature in the room was equivalent to a desert causing him to sweat profusely. The heat lamp made his mouth extremely dry too.

"There is blood in the refrigerator over there," the voice said from an intercom.

Grant looked toward the door thinking he would see someone there to help him then realized the voice came from a speaker in the ceiling. *Great, kidnapped again.* He crawled to the refrigerator and grabbed two bags of blood and popped the first bag on his fangs. He leaned against the wall and closed his eyes savoring the moisture on his dehydrated tongue.

"How do you feel, Grant?" the voice asked from the intercom.

"How in the hell do you think I feel? What did you do to me? Where am I?" Grant yelled up to the speaker as he pounded his chest.

Grant looked around the room for clues. The room was like a small jail cell but with top notch security features. He knew his every move was being watched, but why? He saw the now empty bags of blood and saw the Cantonelli Crest symbol on each bag. *I've been imprisoned in my own home.* Images flashed in his mind of seeing Elise in a wedding dress, then a ceremonial drink from a chalice to then being forced to the floor as his body was filled with rage and hatred. He just didn't understand why.

"I can see that you are upset but please realize we are only doing this for your protection, brother" Santiago said with heartache.

"Santiago?" Grant asked feeling betrayed.

"Yes, Grant. It is me. We have orders from Roman to keep you away from Elise and the baby. I am sorry this is happening" Santiago said.

"Why can't I be with my new wife? I don't understand."

Grant stood up carefully to make sure his balance was okay before running to the steel door to pound on it demanding to be released.

Suddenly, the door unlocked and slid open to show Veronica standing at the door with glowing purple eyes. She had blood smeared all over her clothes, arms, and face as if she had just been in a war. Seeing and smelling the blood made him feel enraged as if he wanted to attack her. Sensing the plan was working she proceeded with her orders from Roman.

He could feel his body taken over by her and was now at her command. Veronica ordered Grant to lay down in the bed and restrain himself with the leather cuffs hanging on each side of the bed. She walked closer to him seeing that he was properly secured then released her control of him and gave the all clear for Roman to enter the room.

Roman boastfully entered the room prepared to attack or defend himself against his business partner and future Grand Vampire trainee. He never let his guard down around an immortal plagued by a charm. Grant felt instant relief when he saw Roman as he knew Roman would release him.

"Roman, tell them this is all a misunderstanding so I can go be with my wife. I mean no harm to anyone. I don't know why I am being held against my will and having my body and mind controlled. I did not agree to this after choosing the immortal lifestyle," Grant said in frustration.

"Calm down. I know you would never voluntarily hurt anyone but a charm has been placed on you therefore we have no choice to restrain you," Roman said as he sifted through Grant's mind for any other clues regarding the charm.

"At least somebody believes me. Get me out of these restraints so I can see Elise," Grant said as he pulled on the leather cuffs.

"I will let you speak to Elise however you will have to stay in restraints as a training exercise for Veronica." Roman said as a lie.

"This is ridiculous," Grant said shaking his head in annoyance.

Roman received a telepathic message from Bart that they were ready to begin the test. He responded silently giving the okay to begin. Veronica and he stood alert and ready while a dozen enforcers waited behind the door.

"Sweetheart, I miss you" Elise's voice announced through the intercom.

Grant's purple eyes began to glow and he transitioned into a raging assassin. His strength increased and his voice changed into something dark and distant. He ripped off the leather cuffs as if it was paper and lunged after Veronica pinning her by her neck against the wall. She felt instant pain but did not make a sound looking to Roman for help. Roman sent a message to all female enforcers to enter Grant's room then ordered all male enforcers to Elise's room to protect her.

"Please don't hurt me. I love you," Elise's voice pleaded on the intercom.

Hearing Elise's voice agitated Grant even more and he began punching Veronica in the stomach. She fell to the floor and protected herself in a fetal position hoping the beatings wouldn't last long. Roman used mind control on Veronica to help ease the pain and calm her during the traumatic experience. He could not physically help her as the actions of the charm needed to play out in order for it to expire. Roman developed a scheme to trick the charm inside Grant into thinking he was successfully completing his mission of killing Elise and the baby. It seemed Roman's plan was working, however Veronica's life was on the line.

"The plan is working. Play the rest of the recording of Elise's voice and crank up the heat lamp," Roman shouted over the radio to Kieron.

Veronica had volunteered to be the bait to try eliminating the charm inside Grant. She knew that her body would go through a serious beating and no matter how much pain she felt, she could not release a sound. Not a whimper, whine or cry otherwise Grant's charm would realize it was not Elise that it was killing. Kieron was able to merge all of Elise's song recordings into messages to use as conversation to Grant so he thought Elise was physically in the room and he was attacking her. Dr. Rowland had taken some blood from Elise to smear all over Veronica as an added measure enticing Grant into thinking Veronica was Elise. It was a far-fetched plan and a lot of risk was involved but the Vampire Council approved.

All twelve female enforcers entered the room in tactical gear and circled around Grant. Their orders were to simultaneously use mind control to help the charm exit from Grant's body and to keep redirecting him under the heat lamp to help evaporate it faster.

"You are hurting the baby," Elise's voice played from the intercom.

Grant pounded on Veronica's head and stomach until she went unconscious. He slowly backed away as the mind control caused him to be disorientated. Grant stumbled backwards holding his head until he fell on his side, face to face with Veronica (Elise) noticing she was dead, which meant the baby was dead. Mission complete. Grant lay on the floor motionless unable to blink or move as the charm removed itself. The charm emerged a glowing ball of fire from his mouth then evaporated in the air.

Four enforcers rushed to aide Veronica in getting her to Dr. Rowland to begin assessing her injuries. She moaned as they stabilized her neck then gently lifted her trying not to injure her any further. They were worried her neck was broken and she had severe internal bleeding based on what they saw Grant do to her. Roman sent a telepathic message to Bartholomew for him to meet Veronica in the hospital room as he knew a romance just recently blossomed between the two.

Grant moaned as he was on the verge of passing out. His eyes rolled in the back of his head and his body shook uncontrollably, having a seizure. Three enforcers moved him to a safer place in the room away from walls or anything that could injure him more, waiting for him to come out of it. Roman told the enforcers to stay with him until he was no longer a threat and quickly left the room to check on Elise and Veronica.

****

The gate watchman notified Roman when the doctors arrived at the estate and he quickly greeted them at the door to usher them to Elise. Three immortal OB/GYN doctors were summoned to the Grand Vampire for a confidential medical case and they were not allowed to ask any questions. Their orders were to pack all medical equipment they would need to assist a mother and baby. Dr. Vornik is a female Russian doctor who specializes in premature births. Dr. Seco is a male Canadian doctor who specializes in births involving a charmed mother and fetus. Dr. Trinchel is a male doctor from Greeneland who specializes in labor and care of the mother prior to birth. Each doctor was amazed to meet the Grand Vampire and was honored to be called upon in a time of need. They signed a confidentiality contract on the helicopter before arrival and knew if the best of care was not provided they could lose their license and possibly be relinquished.

"Dr. Rowland, your help has arrived. Can you get them up to speed with what you know so far about my niece and her son? Veronica is your new around the clock patient," Roman ordered, then quickly went to Veronica's hospital bed.

He approached the door but hesitated to enter. Bartholomew was inside visiting her and Roman could hear every thought and comment. He was holding her hand and crying thinking about the day he first met her and how he finally found his soulmate and was scared to death of losing her. He had planned on taking her to the Alps over a weekend once Elise was out of danger. Now, he didn't know if his best friend or future wife would make it. Bartholomew told Veronica she did not have to volunteer to be the bait person but she would not listen. She insisted on being the person to pretend to be Elise in order to protect the future Grand Vampire's son and her lover's best friend. He understood that she was a trained enforcer and the immortal crisis but could not understand why of all people, his soulmate was the bait. Roman felt his pain as he too had lost his soulmate two hundred years ago.

"You can come in, boss" Bart said.

Roman slowly walked in and put his hand on Bart's shoulder.

"How is she," he asked.

"Doc put her in a medically induced coma to relieve the swelling in her brain. Her stomach was injured so bad he doesn't know if she will get to have children but is praying her body heals it all," Bart said in a cracked voice holding back the tears.

Roman was shocked to hear the possibility Veronica would never have a chance at motherhood because of protecting another woman's baby. Her service to him and the Vampire Council would not go unnoticed.

"I am honored to have her on my team and will provide any resources to assist in her recovery. You are like a son to me, Bartholomew and I do not like to see you hurting. You should be proud of the bravery she has shown today. She is a warrior and will recover from this. I promise you that." Roman said.

"Are you sure, sir? Is this one of your premonitions?" Bart asked, hopefully.

"Put it this way son. I'm paying for your wedding and honeymoon so pick the destination" Roman said as he walked out of the room smiling.

CHAPTER TWENTY

Almost an hour later, Grant woke up to ten enforcers circled around him in the holding cell. He had no memory of what happened and didn't understand why anyone would hurt him. The enforcers read his thoughts and confirmed the charm was completely gone then radioed to all that Mr. Biltmore has been cleared of any charms and Code Shadow is no longer active. While escorting him to Dr. Rowland they told them everything that happened.

All enforcers then escorted the Vampire Council and honorary vampires to a room to be debriefed on what had occurred and the security plans that will remain in place to ensure all safety. Roman spoke to every person to answer any questions and reassure their safety. He announced that the award ceremony will go on as planned the next evening promptly at seven and formal attire was required. He was not going to let Rogue vampires ruin everything. The Vampire Council was pleased how Roman and his team handled the situation but they also had people investigating who "spiked the punch" so to speak. It was decided that the Council would return to Prague after the ceremony to continue business as usual.

Everyone felt horrible that this happened on Grant and Elise's wedding night and that the life of a baby foretold in prophecy books hung in the balance. The future of mortals and immortals living together peacefully may not ever happen which would kill the world faster with violence, hatred, and rage.

Roman went to his office and called Kieron directly.

"Hello?" Kieron asked.

"What was it that you did not want to mention in front of everyone regarding the camera surveillance?" Roman asked intrigued.

"Sir, I don't know how to say this but the intruder that placed the charm on the blood was someone that you know" he said reluctantly.

"Just say it, Kieron" Roman said agitated.

"Sir, it was your brother. Elise's father, Titus." Kieron said apologetically.

****

Elise rested in her hospital bed as she was hooked up to an IV with the Cantonelli crested blood siphoning from a bag to her veins. The three new doctors were busy reading test results, performing their physical assessments and comparing notes with each other. They concluded that the charm did not harm her physically and if it did her body already healed itself prior to their arrival. Her body was functioning normally except for the fact she would not wake up. They explained to Roman that it's as if her body switched to auto pilot and would remain dormant until the charm was cleared from her. Since she was pregnant the red heat lamp could not be used as it was on Grant. The baby seemed to be ok and resting peacefully however they would not know if the charm affected the brain stem until the baby was born and could be properly screened. Roman tried to sift through Elise's thoughts to assess if the baby was in jeopardy however he was blocked. He asked Creighton to try to read her mind as he was older. Unfortunately, he only saw blackness which meant Elise or the charm was blocking their efforts.

Roman held a meeting in the conference room with all remaining forty-three enforcers. He would not release the extra enforcers until the Vampire Council safely returned to Prague after the award ceremony. His main priority was to protect his family and the Council from any Rogues, and his son.

"Thank you all for your hard work against our enemies during this crucial time however we are not in the clear yet. I can confirm that Mr. Biltmore is no longer under the influence of a charm and is recovering in our hospital suite. My niece remains in a coma state however is under the care of very experienced doctors from all around the world. As you know her pregnancy has brought a ray of hope for our immortal community as it was prophesized from our beloved ancestors to be our answer that brings our world together with the humans. I know we all have made friends with mortals throughout our lifetime and had to keep your immortality a secret. Imagine a world of no secrets and being able to live without being worried about our safety from the humans!" Roman said as he addressed the enforcers in an effort to not give up hope.

Many of the enforcers nodded their head in agreeance and some shed tears as they thought about mortal friends they made in their life but could never fully have a close relationship due to their vampire lifestyle. The enforcers were willing to risk their own lives to save the baby that would change the world.

"I ask you to remain vigilant against the Rogues especially to this man on the screen above me. His name is Titus Cantonelli and is to be considered very dangerous." Roman announced with a lump in his throat.

The whole room gasped as they realized it was Roman's brother and Elise's father that was the person responsible for the charm attack. Roman's personal enforcers ordered silence in the room in respect for Roman as he became visibly angry.

"I don't care if you hear a damn twig break, call it in! If you see a damn squirrel run across the wires above the estate, call it in!" Roman shouted as he pointed to several enforcers.

****

Lucas and Santiago sat with Grant in his hospital room as Dr. Rowland took blood and assessed his needs. They were ordered by Roman to stay with the Biltmore family for any emotional support and was officially off duty to be available for their friend.

"I can't believe this is happening. I am going to kill the bastard that did this to us, let alone an innocent child." Grant said is despair as he paced back and forth.

"Calm down, brother. We have plenty of people on it" Lucas said.

"I need to see Elise. Take me to her" Grant said.

Dr. Rowland gave Grant permission to be discharged however wanted to see him back in two days to run another set of blood testing. He expressed how glad he was that Grant was okay and promised to do whatever he could to help Elise and the baby. The Ortega brothers walked with Grant to Elise's room and studied his face when he first saw Elise.

She rested like sleeping beauty waiting for her prince's kiss to awaken her from the deep slumber. Her hair, makeup and nails was still freshly done from their wedding and he broke down in tears. His friends rushed in to comfort him and give him uplifting words until he gained composure and asked for a minute alone with his wife. They left Grant alone and decided to check on Veronica.

Grant lifted Elise's hand and caressed her soft skin before gently kissing each finger. He stood up and leaned over her bed to rub her face then kissed her forehead. He needed to see her purple eyes just like the first time he met her. He couldn't believe how beautiful she was and that he was the lucky man she fell in love with.

"Elise, darling. It's me. I am so sorry this happened to us and lovebug. I will not rest until I find the person responsible for this. Please wake up so I can kiss my bride." Grant said lovingly.

Hoping his words would rouse her awake he sat on the edge of the bed hoping for a response. He lowered his head in disappointment and saw the baby bump on her belly. It had only been a couple of hours since he had seen her and her roundness doubled in size. He was shocked and excited at the same time knowing he would be a father soon. He rubbed her belly back and forth then leaned in close.

"Hey there lovebug, daddy is waiting for you. Keep growing and get stronger so we can play some baseball, huh." He whispered.

He jerked his hand back all of a sudden as her belly began to move from the baby kicking. It was a weird experience and he didn't know what it was doing so he called for help and Dr. Trinchel rushed in.

"What is it sir?" she asked.

"Something is wrong with the baby. Look at her stomach moving around like that." He said in shock.

The doctor chuckled then explained that the baby was growing and moving around more and ensured him that nothing was wrong.

"If the baby was not moving like that it would be worrisome. Are you hoping for a boy or a girl, sir?" the doctor asked.

"I haven't really thought about it. Either would be nice as long as they play baseball." Grant smiled as he rested his palm on her stomach again.

The smiling doctor patted his shoulder and left the room to give them some more privacy. Grant felt a hard kick from the baby against his hand and he realized he loved this baby more than anything in this world and would do anything to protect it. He rose up from the bed and gave her a kiss and quickly left the room.

****

Grant rushed into Roman's office and found him sitting at his desk looking at a photo. He was drinking brandy which was unusual for him to do. Roman seemed startled and shoved the photo into a desk drawer then rose from his seat to hug his business partner.

"Grant, how are you son?" Roman asked.

"I'm good as new and want to kill the person who did this." Grant said as he took a seat.

"Yes, I imagine you do. It's complicated." Roman replied.

"What's complicated about using all resources to bring them back here for a torturous beat down?" Grant said in determination.

Roman sat back down at his desk as he gulped down the once full glass of brandy.

"You wouldn't understand!" he shouted as he slammed the glass back down on his desk.

Grant hadn't seen this vulnerable temperament from Roman before and saw he was deeply troubled. It must have had something to do with the photo he was looking at when he walked in.

"Who is in that photo, Roman?" Grant asked.

"He is my brother Titus when he was four years old trying to ride my horse. He always was the mischievous stubborn type. Insisting on learning everything on his own. You know our parents hired trainers to teach him how to ride and he refused their help saying he could learn on his own." Roman said as he thought of old memories.

"Sounds like he's head strong like his brother," Grant said with a smile.

Roman's smile slowly faded as he realized his brother would not give up until his mission was completed. He then felt guilt, anger, and shame as he thought about the day his brother disobeyed the family and became a Rogue. He just would not listen to anything Roman tried to teach him about the evil Rogues created for mortals and the trouble they caused for vampires in general.

"What is wrong, Roman?" Grant asked.

"What's wrong is that my brother is responsible for putting the charm on you. Also, for putting a charm on his own daughter." Roman said as he watched Grant's reaction.

"You mean to tell me your brother did this not only to his daughter but soon to be grandbaby?" Grant asked in denial.

"I am certain it was him. Kieron got him on video in the garden terrace during the rush of getting the wedding set up. I can't believe what a disgrace he has caused on this family." He said.

"Why would he do this?" Grant asked.

"The Rogues." Roman said as he left the room and the conversation.

Grant went to chase after him when Bart entered the room.

"Grant, its Elise. She's awake!" he said in excitement.

CHAPTER TWENTY ONE

"I can't believe those purple eyes. I know all immortals have them but there is something different about yours, my purple haven." Grant said as he stroked her cheeks and kissing her lips.

"You are too cute for words," Elise said as she chuckled to see him so giddy.

"I was so worried that you would be angry at me. Honey, I didn't know about the charm in the chalice," Grant said to reassure her.

"I believe you, sweetheart. How's lovebug?" she asked.

Grant was about to ask for one of the doctors when all three walked into the room.

"Wow, let me guess. My uncle flew in doctors from all around the world." She said with a smile of his thoughtfulness.

"That would be correct, Mrs. Biltmore." Dr. Seco answered.

Elise loved the sound of hearing Mrs. Biltmore rolling off people's tongues. Ms. Cantonelli was no more as just yesterday she became Grant's wife.

"How are you feeling? Do you feel any pain?" Dr. Vornik asked with concern.

"I feel no pain and I can feel the baby moving. So, all is good right?" Elise asked.

"We have been watching you closely since we arrived this morning and based on our calculations you could go into labor very soon. If you feel any sharp pains or you begin to lose the desire for blood you need to let us know immediately. Do you understand?" Dr. Vornik explained.

Grant became worried at the doctor's tone of voice like something could be wrong. Elise read his thoughts and she too became worried.

"Don't you think it is too early for the baby to come just yet?" Elise asked.

"Mr. and Mrs. Biltmore I do not mean to cause you unrest but our experience with immortal births and charms usually suggest the mother will give birth the day she awakens from the deep sleep caused by the effects of the charm still being in your body." Dr. Vornik said, reluctantly.

****

At the award ceremony, Roman had just finished giving a medal to the last recipient when he received a message from Bartholomew that Veronica was recovered and wanted to report to duty. Roman approved her request and asked for him to bring her to the ceremony.

The Vampire Council was in attendance and sitting in the first row of chairs as they waited patiently for Veronica to arrive. She entered the room holding hands with Bart then quickly stood alert and ready for her next orders.

"Veronica Patelona please come to the front of the room." Roman said out loud.

She was not sure what Roman would request of her and she wanted to look good in front of the Council. Bart sat down in the last row of chairs with a camera and began recording per Roman's request. Creighton rose from his chair and approached the microphone holding a scroll.

"I shall read you a script from the red shield scroll written over five thousand years ago in which is used to honor the most exquisite act of bravery unbeknownst to an immortal. Please know that this was not a planned award however the events that unfolded yesterday prompted this much deserved honor. To the brave who sacrificed their own for another, to the challenger who beat the enemy at all costs, and to the loyal who served with unfaltering resolve. This red shield of honor is awarded to you on behalf of the Vampire Council.

Wear it proudly as the future enforcers can work to achieve what you have done today." Creighton said as he rolled up the scroll.

Creighton pinned the shield on her collar and shook her hand then posed for Bart to take a picture. Roman then gave her a hug and posed with her for a photo. The enforcers cheered as one of their own just experienced the greatest honor. Silence fell as Grant pushed Elise into the room in a wheelchair so she could see her best friend receive the award and thank her for saving her life and the baby's. Veronica burst into tears as she saw Elise with the swollen belly of the prophesized baby she took a beating to protect. She bent over and hugged Elise so tight and they cried together. Elise thanked her for everything she did to get the charm released in Grant. Veronica kissed the tips of her fingers and placed her fingers on Elise's swollen belly. She then stood up straight and looked at Grant apprehensively until Grant also hugged her and apologized for hurting her so badly and explained it was not him, but the charm. He wanted her to be sure she knew he would never consciously hurt her.

Suddenly, Elise cried out in pain and grabbed her stomach then she watched as her hospital gown became soiled with blood.

"Someone help me!" Elise called out then grabbed Grant's hand as a hard contraction paralyzed her body with pain.

"Get her down to the hospital now! Enforcer Team One get the Council safely to their jet. All other enforcers form a barrier line around the whole estate. Don't even let a blade of grass get in between your bodies, baby is coming!" Roman ordered.

Roman and the Council huddled together in conversation as the enforcers loaded all of the Council member's luggage in cars waiting outside. Creighton sent a telepathic message to Roman and blocked his mind to all other immortals in the room so they did not hear. This is an ancient scroll with powerful words that can erase immortal existence all of the world. If Rogues get to that baby, you must be strong enough to use it in order to protect all humanity. Our immortal ancestors created this scroll as a backup plan when the baby was prophesized and the Rogues never knew of it's existence. Creighton reluctantly handed Roman the ancient scroll and told him to only use it if plans do not go accordingly. Roman's hand shook as it was now in his possession.

"Sir, I have suspicious activity located at the south end of the estate. Backup is requested," Bartholomew radioed to Roman.

The enforcers heard the radio traffic and quickly got the guests in the cars and sped off to the airplane hangar. The jet was on standby and waiting for their arrival for takeoff.

"Team two, go to Bartholomew's location and assist. All other enforcers stay in barrier formation until the threat is over, Roman ordered.

*****

Elise was rushed back to her hospital room and all four doctors rushed to her side to assess her. She was dilating fast and she was losing a lot of blood causing her go in and out of consciousness. They hooked her up to an IV of bagged blood and prepared bags of blood for the baby to drink when he came out.

"Will someone please tell me what is happening with my wife, "Grant said panicked as everyone was busy with different tasks.

"Mr. Biltmore, your son is coming very rapidly. Look at you all disheveled. You don't want to greet your son into the world like this. Let me clean you up," Dr. Rowland said as he fixed Grant's collar and adjusted his tie.

Grant was in a daze as Dr. Rowland helped him look good for the happy occasion. He watched Elise rock back and forth in pain in between feeling woozy from losing so much blood. Suddenly she felt the pain slowly recede and yelled out for Grant to come hold her hand. Dr. Trinchel's eyes were purple as he had begun control of her pain level. He stood far back out of the way so the other doctors could work around him as he had control of Elise.

"Grant, no matter what happens please don't let the Rogues get lovebug. Promise me. If they come you must hide him far away and protect him. Do you promise?" Elise pleaded with her husband.

"I'm not leaving you, Elise. Stop thinking negatively and nothing bad will happen. Your pain level seems to be better since the mind control," Grant said trying to distract her.

Roman appeared in the doorway and demanded an update on Elise's condition from the doctors. He saw that she was under mind control for the pain and that pleased him. He did not want her to endure anymore pain than what she had already gone through.

"Uncle, are the enforcers keeping the attacker and Rogues away?" she asked.

"You let me worry about them. You focus on bringing your son into the world, my niece," Roman said as he sat next to her bedside.

"OK everyone. I need the room clear of all visitors except for the father. Elise's body is healing so rapidly that her dilation is receding. We need to act fast," Dr. Seco announced.

Grant stood beside his wife smiling in excitement to see his son for the first time. He kissed her quickly before the doctors got her in position to deliver.

Roman kissed his niece on the forehead and reassured her that the estate was protected to not worry. He stood outside in the hallway waiting patiently to hear the cries of his nephew. He radioed to all enforcers that the time has come for the baby to be born when he received a premonition that shocked him to the core. He heard cries coming from inside the room and was about to rush in when Grant met him at the door and said, "It's not one baby, but two!"

Dear Friends,

I hope you enjoyed this book as much as I had writing it. This was my first jump into paranormal romance genre. I have found this genre to be very addicting!

I want to take a moment and thank the people who have helped make this book possible. To my husband and children, thank you for allowing me the time to pursue my dreams. I hope my works are available as a time capsule for the family generations to come. Although, vampires may not be as popular then as they are now!

I would like to thank my friend, Alisha for editing and expressing your enthusiasm. Nothing better than a high school English teacher to critique work!

I would also like to thank my friend, Dr. Jennifer Gabbard for providing medical terminology and informing me that the blood work outcome could not actually happen in real life. I was just using my imagination, Jen. Congratulations on your rising success!

Love,
Angel

Also Available:

Essence of Time (The Essence Trilogy) Book One

Coming Soon
Essence of Love (The Essence Trilogy) Book Two
Essence of Family (The Essence Trilogy) Book Three

The Ghost Box
Cantonelli's Crest: Special Ops (Kieron's story)

"Like" Angel for instant updates on her Facebook page, Author Angel Musk and visit her website <u>www.angelmusk.com</u> for further information.

Printed in the United States
By Bookmasters